"Don't you think you can control yourself in here alone with me?" he asked in a teasing voice.

"I'm the one who should be asking you that," she said, snapping out the words. Too late, she wished she hadn't, when she saw the darkening in his eyes. The look he was giving her had her pulse beating erratically at the base of her throat.

"Since you brought it up," he said, his gaze roaming her figure from head to toe. "I was going to be a gentleman and control myself, but now I don't think I will."

She backed up and lifted her chin. "You think you're going to force me to do something against my will?" she asked.

He smiled that sexy smile of his and she knew she'd lost the battle already. That darn dimple did her in. "No, but I may force you to admit something you're being rather stubborn about. Although our relationship goals in life are different right now, at this very moment in time we want each other and there is no way you can deny it."

"I do deny it."

"Let's see for how long."

Books by Brenda Jackson

Kimani Romance

Solid Soul
Night Heat
Risky Pleasures
In Bed with Her Boss
Irresistible Forces
Just Deserts
The Object of His Protection
Temperatures Rising

Kimani Arabesque

Tonight and Forever
A Valentine Kiss
Whispered Promises
Eternally Yours
One Special Moment
Fire and Desire
Something to Celebrate
Secret Love
True Love
Surrender

Silhouette Desire

**Delaney's Desert Sheikh*
**A Little Dare*
**Thorn's Challenge*
Scandal Between the Sheets
**Stone Cold Surrender*
**Riding the Storm*
**Jared's Counterfeit Fiancée*
Strictly Confidential Attraction
Taking Care of Business
**The Chase Is On*
**The Durango Affair*
**Ian's Ultimate Gamble*
**Seduction, Westmoreland Style*
***Stranded with the Tempting Stranger*
**Spencer's Forbidden Passion*
**Taming Clint Westmoreland*
**Cole's Red-Hot Pursuit*
**Quade's Babies*
**Tall, Dark... Westmoreland!*

*Westmoreland family titles
**The Garrisons

BRENDA JACKSON

is a die "heart" romantic who married her childhood sweetheart and still proudly wears the "going steady" ring he gave her when she was fifteen. Because she's always believed in the power of love, Brenda's stories always have happy endings. In her real-life love story, Brenda and her husband of thirty-seven years live in Jacksonville, Florida, and have two sons.

A *New York Times* and *USA TODAY* bestselling author of more than fifty romance titles, Brenda is a recent retiree who worked for thirty-seven years in management at a major insurance company. She divides her time between family, writing and traveling. You may write to Brenda at P.O. Box 28267, Jacksonville, Florida 32226; e-mail her at WriterBJackson@aol.com or visit her Web site at www.brendajackson.net.

BRENDA JACKSON

Temperatures Rising

To the love of my life, Gerald Jackson, Sr.

To the Mother Nature Matchmakers' author team—
Carmen Green and Celeste O. Norfleet.
I enjoyed working with you ladies on this one.

To everyone who will be joining me on the 2009
Cruise to Canada. This one is for you!

KIMANI PRESS™

Recycling programs
for this product may
not exist in your area.

ISBN-13: 978-0-373-86112-5
ISBN-10: 0-373-86112-5

TEMPERATURES RISING

www.kimanipress.com

Printed in U.S.A.

Dear Reader,

When I was asked to participate in this MOTHER NATURE MATCHMAKER miniseries, I jumped at the chance. I live in Florida and one thing a Floridian knows about is how forceful a hurricane can be, as well as how to get prepared for it. And wouldn't you know it, parts of this book were written by candlelight when Hurricane Fay decided to blow into town. How ironic is that?

I had fun teaming up with fellow authors Carmen Green and Celeste O. Norfleet to work on this miniseries and write Terrence Jeffries and Sherri Griffin's story. Terrence was first introduced in my March 2009 Silhouette Desire story, *Tall, Dark... Westmoreland!*, as the brother of Olivia Jeffries, my heroine in that story. Terrence, a football legend known as the "Holy Terror," is a man who has no qualms about going after what he wants. Bottom line is that he wants Sherri. But first, together, they have to weather the storm, and that isn't an easy thing for two strong-willed individuals. Trust me when I say this is a man-versus-nature book in a number of ways.

When I was writing this story, I ate a lot of snack foods while sitting up at night listening to my battery-operated radio when the power went out. I appreciated the DJ who kept everyone sane while the heavy rains and strong winds ripped through the city. Terrence is that type of disc jockey. He is also a man determined to win over the woman he loves.

I hope you enjoy Terrence and Sherri's story. The third Jeffries sibling, Duan Jeffries, will be featured in a book now-titled *Spontaneous,* which will be a Harlequin Blaze release in May 2010.

Happy reading!

Brenda Jackson

He that troubleth his own house shall inherit the wind
and the fool shall be servant to the wise of heart.
—*Proverbs* 11:29

Chapter 1

"Sherri, I would be honored if you joined me for dinner at my club tonight."

Sherri Griffin never, ever got headaches, not in all her twenty-seven years. At least not until recently, when she'd taken the job of producer and program director of WLCK, a Key West radio station. That was when she had encountered Terrence Jefferies, a former NFL player for the Miami Dolphins and one of the station's sports commentators.

He was also the owner of Club Hurricane, a popular nightclub in the Keys frequented by celebrities. From what she'd heard, when Terrence began playing pro football he had been nicknamed the Holy Terror by sportscasters because of his oftentimes surly attitude on the field. Besides Mean Joe Greene, there had not been another defensive tackle that had been so respected and feared. But when it came to pursuing women, he used an entirely different strategy. He was all smooth and debonair and never came across as intimidating or bad. Just relentlessly determined.

The man was also handsome as sin.

Drawing in a deep breath, she pulled herself together before looking up from the document she was reading to acknowledge Terrence's entry into her office. Her answer today would be the same one she'd given him yesterday, the day before and for the past few weeks. Little did he know, it would take more than a gorgeous face, broad shoulders and tight buns to make her change her mind. She had to admit, though, there was definitely something about muscle shirts and jeans that clearly defined a well-built male body.

"Thanks for the invitation, but I'll be busy," she responded.

He simply smiled, and that softening around his lips actually sharpened her senses…as if they weren't keen enough already where he was concerned. "One of these days I'm going to follow you home to find out just how you're spending your evenings," he said in a deep and throaty voice.

Definitely without you in them, she thought, wondering if perhaps she was making a mistake by avoiding him, as her best friend, Kimani Cannon, claimed. According to Kim, whenever the Holy Terror made a pass, any normal woman would run with it and rush for the goal line, not turn away like she constantly did. Kim thought the man was as gorgeous as any man had a right to be, and wildly sexy. Grudgingly, Sherri could only admit Kim was right.

But Terrence also had a reputation a mile long, one she would never be able to tolerate. She hadn't been at the station a week when his breakup with some wealthy socialite had been plastered all over the front page of the *Key West Citizen*.

"Sherri?"

She returned her attention to him, wishing he wouldn't say her name like that. Doing so always caused her to remember him in her dreams. And yes, she would admit she'd dreamed about the infuriating man a few times, but as far as she was concerned that meant nothing...other than the fact that she was a woman who could appreciate a stunning male with definite sex appeal.

She placed the documents in her hand down on her desk as she met his gaze. "How I spend my evenings shouldn't concern you, Terrence."

He smiled again and she tried like heck to ignore the little shivers that ran down her spine. The man had a dimple in his right cheek, for heaven's sake! She let out a sigh. He was getting to her, and dimple or no dimple, she was determined not to let him. She knew getting her into his bed was all a game to him—a game of conquest that she had no intention of playing.

"And what if I said I wanted to make it my concern?" he asked, sitting on the edge of her desk and leaning in close.

She tried to ignore the clean and manly aroma of his aftershave. "In that case I would say you have more time and energy than you really need. You might want to channel them elsewhere."

She watched as his mouth—more specifically, his sinfully sculpted lips bordered by a neatly trimmed mustache and beard—eased into a grin. The grin showed his dimple again. She let out a slow breath. If she thought his smile was sexy, then his grin was guaranteed to take a woman's breath away.

"I've been trying to channel them elsewhere for about a month now," he said in a way that told her he still wasn't getting her message. "From the moment I first laid eyes on you I decided to channel all my thoughts, my time and my energy solely on you."

Sherri could only stare at him and wonder if he ever ran out of pick-up lines. Reluctantly, she would even admit he was good at delivering them. It was a good thing that, thanks to Ben Greenfield, she was immune. "Don't waste your time, Terrence."

He shook his head and chuckled, and just like the smile and grin before them the chuckle was explosive. She could feel goose bumps forming on her arm. "It will be time worth wasting," he said, leaning in closer.

She wished she could tell him that she was technically the boss of the radio station and that he was an employee. But she knew that wouldn't work. Terrence and the station's owner, Warrick Fields, were good friends and Terrence's contract stipulated he reported only to Warrick. Everyone's job was to keep the Holy Terror happy, especially since his show received high ratings each week and pulled in huge sponsorships. There was even talk of the show going into syndication next year.

It didn't help matters that Warrick Fields was her mother's twin brother. He had taken her complaints about Terrence with a grain of salt, which proved in this case blood wasn't thicker than water. Uncle Warrick actually thought Terrence's "innocent" flirtation was amusing.

"I can see your mind is busy at work," Terrence said, interrupting her thoughts. "I appreciate a woman who enjoys mulling over things, but now it's you who's wasting time. You can't deny this chemistry between us."

No, she couldn't deny it. Nor would she act on it. "I hate to rush you off, Terrence, but as you can see I have plenty to do."

He glanced at her desk. "I'm going to have to talk to Warrick about that. He shouldn't work you so hard. You should have playtime."

She rolled her eyes and imagined just what kind of playtime he was talking about. "I don't need you to run interference for me. I can hold my own. Thank you."

"If you're sure," he said, smiling and getting to his feet.

"I'm positive."

"Then I'll let you get back to work."

Sherri let out a relieved breath when he turned and headed toward the door. Just her luck, he stopped before walking over the threshold and turned back around. When he caught her gaze, she felt the thud deep in her chest at the same time a heated sensation traveled down her spine. He stood there in her doorway, all six foot three of him, and she could only stare at the well-built body. And his dark eyes were focused right on her.

"I won't give up, Sherri. I think you know that," he said in a determined tone. Not intimidating, not threatening. Just promising and unwavering.

Yes, she did know that, and the thought that one day he just might succeed made her pulse pound. But she would continue to resist him since getting involved in a relationship was the last thing on her mind. Building a career at the station was her top priority.

She made no response to what he'd said. He really didn't give her a chance since he then turned and walked out the door, closing it behind him. Only then did she lean back in her chair and breathe. His masculine scent lingered in her office and she reached out and touched the spot on her desk where he'd sat. It was hot. The man was so hot-blooded he was capable of leaving heat behind.

He was determined to make trouble and she was just as determined not to let him. She had a job to do. Uncle Warrick was thinking about retiring in another year and he wanted her to be ready to take over as station manager when he did so. She would prove to her uncle that his faith in her was not a mistake, and that she would be more than capable of managing the day-to-day operations of WLCK. Although it seemed the Holy Terror was not going to make her job easy, there was no way she would let him get in the way of her achieving her goal.

She stood and walked to the window and looked out. Key West was a beautiful seaport city and WLCK served the people by being one of the most popular stations in the area. She loved working here.

She had arrived almost a month ago and discovered the radio station that her uncle owned was a nice size compared to others she'd seen. Although the pay scale wasn't any higher, not too many other stations could boast of having an ocean within walking distance.

The first change she had implemented upon taking the job was reinstating the dress code. According to Uncle Warrick, there had always been a dress code, but somewhere down the line the employees had ignored it, reasoning that it didn't matter how they looked since the audience couldn't see them.

Sherri believed in dressing professionally, and in the end she and the staff had compromised. The too-laid-back attire of shorts and flip-flops had gotten ruled out and replaced by business casual, with the majority of the employees wearing jeans and tops.

Personally, she'd never been a jeans-wearing woman. While working around a more aristocratic crowd at her uncle's station in D.C., she had gotten used to business suits. Going from professional to casual wasn't as easy as she'd thought, but she was working on it.

She glanced at her watch and walked back over to her desk. Terrence's sports talk show would be airing in a few minutes and she wanted to tune in. Each office was equipped with an intercom that broadcasted all the shows so you could listen at will. Not that she was all into sports, but she made a habit of tuning in to his show, which filled an hour time slot twice a week.

Flipping on the dial of the radio unit beside her desk, she leaned back in her chair and slipped off her shoes with a long sigh. She'd spend the next hour with Terrence Jefferies. The man who was trying to get next to her—and the man she was determined to ignore.

Terrence couldn't help but smile after hanging up the phone from talking to his sister. Olivia was happy and he was happy for her. It seemed the ugly hands of disaster hadn't caught her in their clutches the way they had his father.

His mother had walked out on his old man, leaving him with the task of becoming a single father with three kids to raise. Terrence had been ten at the time, Duan twelve and Olivia only three. Things might not have been so bad if the man his mother had run off with hadn't had a wife and kid of his own.

He was glad Olivia hadn't listened to their father a few months back when he found out she'd gotten serious about a guy—a guy who just happened to be running against their father for a senate seat in the Georgia General Assembly. She had married Reggie Westmoreland and now she had a man who loved her and a huge family who had embraced her with a warm and sincere welcome.

Terrence glanced at his watch. He had already touched base with Cullen Carlisle, better known as CC, whom he'd hired to manage Club Hurricane a few years ago. According to CC, things were pretty busy for a Tuesday night, which wasn't surprising considering this was the first week in June. Every year at this time college students headed south before making the trip home, wherever home was for them.

So far there had been only one situation where CC, who stood two inches taller than Terrence and weighed close to two-fifty, had had to intervene to bring order. A lamp on one of the tables had gotten broken and the man responsible quickly paid for the damages. Terrence chuckled. Knowing CC, it was either pay up then or have pieces of the broken lamp shoved down your throat. To say CC took his job seriously was an understatement.

Terrence decided to do something he rarely did—be in bed before ten. Might as well since he hadn't managed to talk Sherri into joining him at the club.

Sherri Griffin.

It took a lot for him to admit that he was virtually obsessed with the woman and had been since walking into Warrick's office a month ago and finding her standing there.... Bending over was more like it. She had leaned down to pick a paper clip off the floor. He had appreciated the look of her shapely backside before getting a chance to see her face, and when he had, he had been pleased with the total package.

As he removed the last piece of his clothes to step into the shower, he couldn't help but recall the exact moment she had straightened her body, turned around and looked into his face. He had stood there, literally transfixed while drinking in the lusciousness of her curves before taking an admiring visual path up to her face.

If there was such a thing as instant, mind-blowing physical attraction, he had experienced it right then and there. A woman being pretty was one thing, but being punch-in-the-gut beautiful was another. First there was the most mesmerizing pair of sable-brown eyes he'd ever seen. Then there was a rounded chin on a medium-brown oval face, the two somehow totally in sync with each other. In addition to the softness of her high cheekbones and her shoulder-length styled hair, she had a pair of lips he would have given anything, possibly even his Heisman Trophy, to get a taste of.

Sizzling heat had instantly invaded his body, and it had taken Warrick saying his name twice before he had dragged his gaze away from her. But not before that same gaze had studied her hands and found her fingers ringless. And not before he'd decided that his six months of sexual draught were about to come to an end.

While Warrick had gone about making introductions, Terrence could tell by the set of Sherri's jaw that she hadn't liked the interest he was showing in her and she wouldn't make things easy for him. No problem there since he was a man who appreciated a challenge every once in a while. Trouble was, he hadn't counted on her still being a difficult case almost an entire month later. He refused to believe he was losing his touch or that the physical attraction hadn't been mutual. He had seen the flame that had come alive in her eyes, although she had immediately tried to douse it.

For him, Sherri Griffin projected a number of things and sexual pleasure headed the list. There was something totally feminine and sensually captivating about her. While she tried coming across as all business, he refused to go there with her. The only level he was willing to meet her on was a sexual one. The effect she had on him would make it impossible for things to be otherwise.

So since she wanted to play hard to get, he would start turning up the heat. What the hell. At thirty-four, he still enjoyed having fun and there hadn't been any excitement in his life since finding out about Olivia's involvement with their father's political enemy. And as the warm rush of water trickled over his skin, he quickly came up with a plan to deal with Ms. Griffin.

By the time he got in bed less than an hour later, his body was relaxed and his mind was clear. He didn't intend to overwhelm her or pressure her. Instead, he would use the oldest trick known to a desperate man, one that included seduction that was impossible to resist. He wasn't called the Holy Terror for nothing.

Chapter 2

"I can't believe you turned him down again."

From the top of the stairs, Sherri looked at Kim, who was still standing below with an astounded expression on her face. Three days a week she and Kim met to jog along the beach where their condos were located. After leaning over and inhaling slow and deep, Sherri straightened her body and placed her hands on her hips.

The disappointment in Kim's voice was evident, and Sherri couldn't help wondering why. "Really, Kim, it's not that bad. He'll get over it, but now I'm worried as to whether or not you will. What's with you wanting me to go out with him, knowing his reputation?"

Instead of answering, Kim jogged up the stairs to join her. After taking a huge gulp of water from the water bottle, she said, "Because I know you can handle him."

If only Kim knew just how wrong she was, Sherri thought. She was still reeling from the side effects of that visit he had made to her office two days ago.

"Besides, you need to indulge yourself in a fling," Kim added.

Now it was Sherri whose face was filled with astonishment. She couldn't believe her friend had made such an outlandish statement. "Let me get this right. You think my way to handle him is to have an affair with him?" She saw the smile that lit Kim's features and wasn't all that pleased it was at her expense.

"Hey, get the daggers out of your eyes," Kim said, laughing. "I'm just reminding you of the promise you made to me last year."

Sherri lifted a brow. "And what promise was that?"

"The promise that once you got out here and were settled, you would let go of that situation with Ben Greenfield and concentrate on meeting someone else."

Sherri dragged her eyes away from Kim. "I've been busy," she said, which in a way was true.

Kim wiggled her brows. "Now that reminds me of another promise you've broken, the one where you swore you would never let work interfere with pursuing a worthwhile relationship with a man. Especially because Ben claimed the reason he was breaking off your engagement was that you could never make time in your busy schedule for him, so he—"

"Found someone else," Sherri finished for her softly. At the time she'd felt it had been a lousy excuse for his infidelity. His betrayal had hurt.

"You said you wouldn't give another man the chance to make that claim," Kim reminded her.

"Which is the reason I refuse to get involved with anyone," Sherri said. "I don't have the time right now. I need to learn all I can and—"

"You know all you need to know about running a radio station, Sherri. Come on, this isn't the first one you've managed. All you had to do is become familiar with the setup of WLCK. You're good at what you do," Kim said as they began walking slowly toward Sherri's bungalow.

"Thanks."

"You're welcome. Now back to the reason why you won't go out with the Holy Terror," Kim said while looping her arms around her friend's shoulders.

Sherri couldn't help but smile. Kim refused to let up, and it served Sherri right for convincing her friend to move to the Keys with her when she had gotten the job offer from her uncle Warrick. Since Kim was a nurse, it hadn't been hard for her to get a job at one of the hospitals here.

Sherri had just opened her mouth to say something when she saw the floral arrangement in front of her door. "Wow! I wonder where these came from."

She picked up the vase filled with a beautiful arrangement of mixed flowers. "They're gorgeous, aren't they?"

"Yes, so who sent them?" Kim asked.

Sherri pulled off the card and opened it up. Moments later she massaged the bridge of her nose and closed her eyes, not wanting to believe the message written on the card.

"Well, Sherri, who sent them?"

She opened her eyes and frowned at Kim. "They're from Terrence, like you really wouldn't know," she said.

Kim placed a hand over her mouth in surprise. "The Holy Terror sent you those?"

Sherri lifted her heard and quirked a brow. "Don't tell me you're really surprised about this," she said.

Kim shrugged. "Well, I am. I did my research on the guy and everything I've read about Terrence Jefferies indicates that when it comes to pursuing women he doesn't put out a lot of effort or give it much thought. He doesn't have to since women usually flock to him." She glanced at the floral arrangement. "I would think a lot of thought went into ordering those."

Sherri would think so, too, but then, she hadn't gone to the trouble of doing an investigation of Terrence like Kim had done. "I can't get weakened by this," she decided to say. "I'll thank him for the flowers but make absolutely sure he understands that nothing has changed. I still won't go out with him."

She looked at the flowers and couldn't help but smile.

Her smile faded when she noticed the sympathetic look on Kim's face. Kim knew her better than anyone. "I'm headed for troubled waters, aren't I?" she asked her friend softly.

Kim chuckled. "Yes, and I hope you can swim."

Later that night after taking her shower, Sherri put on her silk bathrobe and then curled up on the sofa with the card she'd received with the flowers. Again she read the message Terrence had written.

Please have dinner with me tomorrow night at my club.
Terrence

The man just wouldn't give up. She wondered what would happen if she refused him again. Would he continue to be persistent? She felt her body tremble at the thought.

During her first week on the job, Terrence had been out of town attending his sister's wedding. But from the moment her uncle Warrick had introduced them, she had felt this pull, this sexual chemistry. Unlike him, she had been willing to ignore it, to move on and place her focus on more important issues like becoming acquainted with the day-to-day operations of the station. But that didn't mean he hadn't crossed her mind a few times or that he wouldn't give her system one hell of a jolt whenever she would run into him in the corridors.

She recalled seeing him at the water fountain one day, and the sight of him bending over and drinking water—how his mouth adjusted to take in the liquid—had made her senses whirl and her blood rush through her veins. And when he'd finished, he had licked his lips. She had been totally embarrassed when he had glanced up and seen her staring at him like a ninny.

She reread his card. The least she could do was call and thank him for the flowers, she thought, glancing across the room at them. She had found the perfect spot, right in front of the window. She had the window open and a soft breeze was flowing through, wafting the fragrance toward her.

Before she changed her mind, she called him.

"Hello."

Even with the noise she could hear in the background, Terrence's deep masculine voice came through the phone loud and distinctively clear. It moved over her skin like a soft caress. "Terrence, this is Sherri."

"I know. Your name popped up," he said, and she could just imagine the potency of the smile he had on his lips.

"Thanks for the flowers. They're beautiful," she rushed on to say, deciding to stick with the reason she'd phoned and end the call.

"You're welcome. I'm glad you like them." There was a pause. Then he asked, "What about dinner? Will you join me tomorrow night here at the club?"

Sherri closed her eyes. In the recesses of her mind, she could actually pick up the scent of his aftershave and could see that enticing smile on his lips, the one that made her feel as if something akin to liquid fire flowed through her veins. She then thought of his body heat, the heat she felt whenever she was around him. The same heat he had left in her office. She opened her eyes when she actually felt the phone tremble in her hands.

She could think of all the reasons she should not have dinner with him. She had gone over them a number of times before, most recently just an hour ago while she was in the shower. In essence, nothing had changed. Yet for some reason she wanted to have dinner with him.

"Yes, I'll join you for dinner," she said quickly, accepting that although nothing had changed, she needed to get beyond this thing with him. Maybe having dinner with him this one time would help her do so.

"All right. Do you want me to pick you up or would you rather we meet here?"

She did not want him to pick her up. Him coming into her home for any reason was something she'd rather avoid. "I can meet you there," she said. "Will six o'clock be okay?"

"Fine. Do you know how to get to Club Hurricane?" he asked.

"Yes. Although I've never been there, I've passed by it a few times. It looks like a real nice place."

"It is. And I look forward to showing you around."

There was something about the way he'd made that last statement that warned her to keep her senses in check while around him. Not doing so would be reckless. "I'll look forward to it. Good night."

"Good night, Sherri."

Sherri clicked off the phone, feeling warm and tingly all through her body. Terrence had a way of making her feel that way, even when he was miles away.

It took a few seconds after disconnecting the call from Sherri for Terrence to remember he had visitors. He glanced across the table at the two men who'd dropped by the club to see him, his best friends Lucas McCoy and Stephen Morales. The three had met while attending the University of Miami and had instantly bonded. Lucas was engaged; his fiancée lived in New York but had agreed to move to Key West after the wedding. He was building a beautiful house for them on his family property.

Stephen, whose birth name was Esteban, was a deputy sheriff. A few years ago he had given up a rather plush job with his father's successful construction company to work with his paternal grandfather, the local sheriff.

"Are we keeping you from your date, Terrence?" Stephen asked, plastering a huge smile on his face.

"Yeah, man, we can check you out later if we're in the way," Lucas followed up by saying.

Terrence returned their gazes, not giving any sign that he was taking either of them seriously. "You're fine. My date isn't until tomorrow night."

"Anyone we know?" Stephen was curious enough to ask.

"No, but eventually you will." After he'd said the words, he wondered why he was so certain. It wasn't as if he intended to make Sherri a permanent fixture in his life. In fact, he intended for anything between them—once it got started—to be short-term. At the moment, she was an itch that needed scratching. Bad.

And when had he ever wanted his two closest friends to meet any woman he was involved with? Things with Vicki Waller had been different because she had somehow gotten it into her head that she would one day become Mrs. Terrence Jefferies, although he had told her time and time again that she wouldn't. Their breakup had made the papers, but only because she had erroneously informed a number of people they were planning to get married.

"So we're still on for this coming weekend?" Lucas was asking, reclaiming his attention. They had made plans to get some boating time in. Forecasters had predicted nice weather.

"Only if you're sure Emma isn't coming to town," Terrence said, referring to Lucas's fiancée. Terrence saw the tightening of Lucas's jaw, and even before his friend spoke he knew what he was about to say. Lucas and Emma had been doing the long-distance-dating thing for almost a year now, but lately it seemed Lucas was traveling more to New York than Emma was coming to Florida.

"I'm sure she won't be coming," was Lucas's terse response.

"Okay, then," Terrence said, reaching out and squeezing Lucas's shoulder. "Our weekend on the water is all set."

"Okay, pal, don't think we're letting you off the hook that easy," Stephen said, grinning. "Who is this woman that just brought a sparkle to your eyes?"

"You're imagining things," Terrence said, rolling those same eyes.

"I don't think so," Stephen countered. "We want a name."

Knowing they wouldn't let up, he said, "Her name is Sherri Griffin. She's Warrick's niece and works at the station as a programmer and producer. However, Warrick's grooming her to be manager when he retires."

"Is she pretty?" Lucas wanted to know.

Terrence didn't say anything for a minute while sipping his drink, and then he said, "She is stunning. I mean jaw-dropping gorgeous, even in her business suits."

Lucas chuckled. "The woman actually wears business suits? Here in the Keys?"

Terrence smiled. "Yes, but I'm sure sooner or later she'll be coming out of them." *And I'm going to make sure she does.*

Later that night Terrence strode through the door of his condo, satisfied that he'd finally gotten Sherri to have dinner with him. Now he had to continue to move forward. Remain calm. Stay in control. Yet he couldn't overlook the same key questions that persistently reared their inquisitive heads. Why did it matter? Why was getting under Sherri Griffin's skin so important to him? Why when he thought of such a thing happening did his heart thump furiously in his chest?

He moved to the window and looked out of it with serious eyes. Intense eyes. And to top it off, warning signals were going off in his head. He was not a man who thrived on escalating relationships. For reasons instilled deep within him, he much preferred affairs that led nowhere, and he certainly never considered the thought or possibility that he would diligently pursue a woman who refused to reciprocate the interest.

Yet he was.

He exhaled deeply as he moved toward his bedroom, fully aware that he still had his work cut out for him. For the moment, he wouldn't spend time questioning why reaching his goal of bedding Sherri Griffin was of vital importance to him.

Chapter 3

Sherri inhaled deeply as she walked through the doors of Club Hurricane. After deciding a change of clothes was in order, she had rushed home from the station to quickly strip off her business suit and shower before slipping into a short pleated skirt and a silk top.

She glanced around and was impressed with the decor of the establishment and its ability to blend both casual and tailored, thanks to a solid wall of glass that provided a panoramic view of the ocean. Immediately she knew she had entered Terrence Jefferies's domain. It was as high-class as the man himself.

She was greeted by a hostess. "Ms. Griffin?"

Sherri was surprised the woman knew her name. "Yes?"

The hostess smiled. "Mr. Jefferies has asked that I escort you to him."

Sherri returned the smile. "All right."

They passed the bar and stage on the way to the part of the club where food was served. Terrence stood there waiting. Sherri's breath caught the moment she saw him, dressed casually in a pair of white linen slacks and matching long-sleeve shirt that hung outside his pants and made him look muscular and toned. Appearances were important, personally and professionally, and he'd cornered the market for both.

"Thank you, Debbie. I'll take over from here," he said, taking Sherri's hand.

Debbie nodded before walking off, leaving Sherri alone with Terrence. He looked at her and smiled. "Thanks for joining me tonight."

She felt the nervous tension in her stomach from just the feel of her hand in his. "Thanks for inviting me," she said.

He then looked down at her from head to toe before returning an appreciative gaze to her face. "You look nice."

"You look nice, as well." And she meant it. He was definitely one fine-looking man.

He tightened his hand around hers. "I promised you a tour, so let me show you around."

"All right."

"The club is really divided into three sections. When you first enter you have the bar with the big screen for sports enthusiasts. There we not only serve drinks but sandwiches, salads and appetizers. The area across from the bar is where the music is set up so it can be heard in all parts of the club."

They stopped walking and he gestured to where the band was still setting up. "We have live music on Tuesdays, Thursdays and the weekends. A huge dance floor separates these two areas from the restaurant, which overlooks the ocean."

She glanced at the huge glass wall that covered the length of the back of the club. "Nice setup."

"Thanks. It was designed to take into consideration all age groups, from the twentysomething up to the fifty-and-over crowd." They walked slowly back to the dining area. "This part of the club is my favorite. I tried capturing the Key West flavor while maintaining a classy opulence," he said proudly.

She glanced over the restaurant. "And I think you succeeded." On each of the mahogany tables sat a hurricane lantern on top of an ocean-blue tablecloth. The chairs, padded with contoured backs, were shaped like seashells. The design of the chairs and the ocean on the other side of the glass window combined to create a seashore atmosphere while maintaining a high level of classiness.

He then gave her a tour of the kitchen and the rest of the club. "What made you decide on the name?" she asked when they returned to the restaurant area.

He smiled. "Two reasons. First, I played football for the University of Miami Hurricanes, and second, this area is susceptible to more hurricanes than any other part of Florida. I was in my first year of college when Hurricane Andrew blew up. Let's just say hurricanes have given me a whole new respect for Mother Nature."

"Hurricanes and all, you do like it here." It was more of a statement than a question.

He chuckled. "Yes, I like it here. I enjoy going back home to visit, but as far as putting down roots, I can't imagine living anywhere else."

He glanced at his watch. "I hope you're hungry," he said, keeping a firm grip on her hand while leading her toward an elevator.

Sherri nervously glanced around. "Yes, but aren't we eating here?"

Another smile touched Terrence's lips. "No. For space and privacy, my suite upstairs will be better. Do you mind?"

She glanced up at him, searched his face for any indication that she should mind. There was still chemistry between them, she couldn't deny that, but she didn't feel threatened at the thought of being alone with him. She forced herself to relax. "No, I don't mind."

They stepped into the elevator, and after Terrence pressed a button, the door closed. She'd never noticed just how intimate the inside of an elevator was until now. Nor had she known how hard it was to resist temptation until now. Terrence stood looking at her but saying nothing. He didn't have to. His eyes said it all.

What she hadn't read in them before stepping into the elevator was clearly in his gaze now. That long-standing desire she had tried to ignore was obvious. Whether it was because he saw her as a challenge or just the new woman on the block that he had to have a piece of, she wasn't sure. But there was no doubt in her mind that he wanted her, and, if given the opportunity, he wouldn't waste any time getting her.

That's where temptation came in. She was tempted to give in to Kim's way of thinking: that her constant rejection of his advances was absurd and that women with their heads screwed on right didn't hesitate to date someone like Terrence. As far as Sherri was concerned, even being here tonight spoke volumes, but she wasn't ready to throw all caution to the wind. She had a tendency to take things slow, wade in the water before actually taking a dive. But still, all she would have to do now was to reach out and touch him. Feel his muscles. Taste that smile right off his lips.

Before desire could play havoc with her common sense, the elevator door swooshed open. His hand touched the center of her back as he led her out of the elevator, and it took everything within her not to moan from his touch. Her breasts suddenly felt tender. Her nipples felt hard against the fabric of her blouse. And the body heat emanating from him was stirring sensations deep inside her.

They stepped off the elevator into a brightly lit hall, and with his hand still firmly placed on her back, he led her to a room that had a balcony facing the ocean and a table for two had been set. Candlelight and soft music told her they would be sharing a romantic evening.

She glanced around and saw a king-size bed against the wall. When her gaze met his, he read the question in her eyes.

"It's needed," he said softly. "On weekends the club stays open until two and it's easier for me to crash here instead of going home. You're free to take a look around and enjoy the view of the ocean from the balcony while I phone the kitchen so they can deliver our food."

She nodded and gave an appreciative glance around the room, making sure her main focus was no longer on the huge bed. As she walked toward the balcony she couldn't help but be impressed. Just like downstairs, the suite was immaculate. The only difference was that the furnishings in here were modern.

"Would you like something to drink while we wait?"

She stopped walking and glanced over her shoulder. He stood there, braced against a table, his eyes unerringly on her. Her body responded. Just that simple. Just that easy. She wondered if he could gauge her response to him. "Yes."

"White wine okay?"

She saw his gaze lower to her legs, and instinctively she smoothed the hem of her short skirt along her thighs. "That would be fine. Thanks." She turned around and continued walking, knowing his eyes watched every step she took. A part of her wished he wouldn't pay so much attention to her body. Then another part, the one that appreciated the fact she was a woman, didn't mind at all; in fact, that part was glad he noticed. He was a man, after all. It would be up to her to stay in control and keep things in perspective.

Before stepping out on the balcony she glanced over at his bed once more, wondering how many women he'd had between those sheets and deciding right then and there that no matter how much sexual magnetism he transmitted, she wouldn't be one of them.

With two wineglasses in his hands, Terrence moved toward the balcony then suddenly stopped when he glanced ahead and saw Sherri. She leaned against the balcony's rail while the wind gently blew in her hair. He sucked in a deep breath, felt his body get hard and quickly decided it would be best to stay just where he was for the time being. No problem. She hadn't noted his presence, which gave him the opportunity to notice hers.

She looked sensational, sexy and hot all rolled into one. She was tall, around five-eight, curvy, with a small waist and dark hair that billowed around her shoulders in soft, bouncy waves. Even now her outfit made sweat bead out on his forehead. She had the perfect legs for her short skirt and the perfect breasts for her low-cut blouse and he would love the chance to taste both legs and breasts. If ever there was a reason to call a woman delectable, then this would be it. He could just envision starting at the soles of her feet and working his mouth upward toward her lips, taking time to fully savor the feminine part of her in between. He knew that degree of lovemaking would come later. Right now he needed to work his way up to a simple kiss.

He smiled then, thinking that when they kissed there wouldn't be anything simple about it. It definitely wouldn't be anything close to a brush across the lips or a light smooch. He intended to make up for lost time. Work his tongue in her mouth in a way that she would know, would always remember, that he had been there.

Sherri turned when she heard the sound of Terrence returning. She took a deep breath and tried to calm herself. He was just a man. A man who, if given the opportunity, could change her life forever…but not for the better. She refused to let that happen. She had given one man total access to her heart and she would never do so again.

"Here you are," he said, handing the glass of wine to her.

"Thanks." She glanced back at the ocean. "This is such a beautiful view from here. So peaceful."

He followed her gaze. "You should be here to see it one morning at sunrise."

She looked at him over the rim of her glass. Was he issuing her an invitation? If so, it was definitely wasted. Instead of responding to what he'd said, she decided to change the subject. "Tell me about Terrence Jefferies."

He lifted a brow. "What do you want to know?"

"Anything you want to tell me."

He took a sip of his wine, and it was a few moments before he spoke. "My family lives in Atlanta. There's my father, my older brother, Duan, who is thirty-six, and my sister, Olivia, who got married last month. Olivia is twenty-seven."

"What about your mom?"

She saw the way his jaw tensed when he said, "I don't have a mother."

She felt bad for asking. Thinking his mother had evidently passed away, she said, "I'm sorry."

He lifted a brow. "Why? You didn't do anything."

"I shouldn't have asked about your mother," she said softly.

He stared back at the ocean before meeting her gaze. "My mother isn't dead, if that's what you're thinking. She and my father split when I was ten, Duan was twelve and Olivia was only three. She gave my father full custody of us, kept walking and never looked back."

"Oh." Sherri didn't know what to say. Her parents were still happily married after thirty years, and she couldn't imagine a woman not keeping in touch with her children. Deciding she needed to change the subject yet again, she said, "How long have you owned the club?"

"About four years. I purchased it right after an injury caused me to stop playing for the Dolphins and I decided to settle here instead of moving back to Atlanta."

"What made you decide to remain in South Florida?"

"Close friends from college, Stephen Morales and Lucas McCoy. We attended the University of Miami together. Stephen is a deputy sheriff and Lucas renovates houses. Another reason I decided to stay is that I like the area, especially the beaches."

As he spoke, she noticed his gaze had shifted from her eyes to her lips. A second of silence passed before he said in a deep, husky tone, "There's something I've wanted to do ever since the first day I saw you."

She fought to quell the sensations flowing through her. "What?"

"This." And then he lowered his head, skimming her lips lightly a few times before capturing them fully with his.

She felt the room tilt when he masterfully deepened the kiss, deliciously tempting her to submission. She moaned when his tongue roamed freely everywhere in her mouth before grasping hold on hers, toying with it, mating with it, feasting greedily on it. Her control crumbled in the intense and sensual assault of his mouth.

She felt the hardness of him pressing against her middle, and at that very moment her senses, the ones still operating, were thrown into overdrive, and her body felt like it was actually overheating. As shards of pleasure cascaded through her, her stomach tensed. Her nipples pressing against his chest ached. Heat flared between her legs and her pulse beat relentlessly.

When he finally pulled his mouth away, she dropped her face to his chest and stifled another moan. Her defenses were all but shattered as the result of one kiss. She hadn't expected it. Hadn't been fully prepared for it. Her mouth had yielded for him in a way it had never yielded for another man.

She lifted her head and met his eyes. The look he gave her was intense. Deep. Sensual. The air surrounding them actually seemed to thicken. She didn't know what sort of tactics he'd used when he played on the football field, but here, right now, he was using his own sensual weapon to advance and he clearly was determined to reach the goal line with her before the night was over. She opened her mouth to tell him that it was not going to happen when she heard a doorbell.

"Our dinner has arrived."

His words filtered through her chaotic mind, and before she could say anything, he had taken her hand and was leading her back inside.

He intended to invade her territory.

Although Terrence figured she wouldn't like it, it would be done. He had gotten a taste of her, a taste that even a full-course meal later, he couldn't let go of.

Their conversation over dinner he'd dismissed as chitchat. She'd told him about being an only child with a lot of cousins and the only one of them interested in following in her uncle's footsteps by working in radio. She'd told him about her best friend, Kim, who had decided to move to the Keys with her. She'd told him how she intended to go shopping for a new car by the end of the year. One thing she hadn't mentioned was her love life, specifically the guy her uncle had mentioned, the one who supposedly had broken her heart last year.

He glanced across the table. After a long, drawn-out silence while they'd enjoyed another glass of wine, he decided to stir up conversation again by coming out and asking point-blank, "Do you engage in affairs?"

From the way her head snapped up and the surprised look on her face, he knew his question had caught her off guard. He watched as she regained her wits and released a long, slow breath. He even felt when the shiver passed through her.

Then he saw a slow smile touch her lips when she said, "I understand that you do."

She hadn't answered his question but had made a comment instead, one he fully intended to answer. "Yes, I do," he murmured truthfully. "Short-term affairs. I don't do long term."

"Commitment phobia?"

"Not necessarily. I just decided very early in life that I would die single. Matters of the heart are not for me."

There was no need to tell her he felt that way because of the pain he'd seen his father endure after his mother had walked out on them for another man, nearly destroying their family in the process. Nor would he mention how as a child he had watched a once happily married man learn to cope as a divorced husband and a single father. A man whose life was filled with pain and sadness and for whom the only thing that mattered in his life was his children. Terrence was convinced to this day that his father had never gotten over the betrayal of his wife.

Just like he had never gotten over the betrayal of his mother.

"Then what about that article I read in the newspaper the first week I arrived? The one about your broken engagement."

He glanced over at her and decided to set the matter straight. "There was never an engagement. I don't ever plan to marry, and she knew it. I can only assume that she was hoping I would change my mind."

Deciding he needed to make sure Sherri fully understood so there would never be any misunderstanding, he held her gaze and then added, "That is one thing I don't intend to ever change my mind about. I will never marry."

Sherri could only nod. Terrence was making his position absolutely clear to her, and she appreciated it because she now knew how to handle him in the future. Virtually the same way she'd been doing in the past. She didn't regret having dinner with him. It had been both enjoyable and enlightening.

It would be easy if she were the type of woman who had no qualms in engaging in the same type of affairs that he did, but she wasn't. Her parents were enjoying a relatively happy marriage, and although at this point in her career, marriage was the furthest thing from her mind, she still wanted the same for herself one day. A man who would love her and cherish her, give her his babies, his life, his world. Terrence had just told her in no uncertain terms that he was not the man for her. He lived for the moment, and the women he dated would never, ever get close to his heart. She wondered if the way his mother had walked out of his life was the reason. In a way, his take on things was no different from Kim's. As a child, she had watched her father physically abuse her mother, and because of it, although Kim did on occasion indulge in what she considered a healthy relationship, she never intended to marry.

Thinking the silence between them had extended long enough, she said, "Thanks again for dinner, Terrence. The steak was delicious. I commend your staff. It was the most incredible meal I've ever eaten."

He smiled at her compliment. "Thanks. We aim to please. I suggest you visit on a Wednesday night. It's ladies' night and our specialty dessert is a key lime pie that is to die for."

A smile touched her lips. "I think I will." She glanced at her watch. "It's getting late. I'm due in at the station rather early in the morning, and I need a good night's sleep."

"You can always stay here for the night."

She took his kindness for what it was. An invite to roll between the sheets with him. "Thanks, but I prefer my own bed," she said, getting to her feet.

"You're sure I can't entice you to enjoy dessert before you leave?" he asked, getting to his feet, as well. His voice was low and husky, making her wonder just what kind of dessert he was talking about. She had a feeling it wasn't anything his cooks could whip up in their kitchen. Rather, the two of them would be stirring up all the ingredients.

"Yes, I'm positive. I do need to leave." *Either that or be tempted to take you up on your offer.* Although she knew where he stood, he was still temptation, the type she was finding it hard to resist. Even now she could feel sexual tension flowing in the air between them, heightening her full awareness of him as a man.

The kiss they had shared hadn't helped matters. A part of her wished she could toss caution to the wind and engage in the type of affair he was used to, but she was too quick to give her heart. An involvement with Terrence would be heartbreak just waiting to happen.

But boy, was she tempted…

"If you're sure that you're ready to leave, I'll walk you down."

His words filtered through her mind and interrupted her thoughts. He was giving her a chance to change her mind, to reconsider his invitation. But she wouldn't. "Thanks, and yes, I am sure."

"All right."

She watched as he rounded the table to walk toward her, and her heart pounded deep in her chest with every step he took. He would escort her down but he intended to kiss her again before he did. She felt it in her bones. She felt his intentions in the very air she was breathing. It was there on his face, in his expression, especially in the eyes that held her in their direct gaze.

She suddenly felt hot, light-headed. When he came to a stop in front of her, saying nothing but concentrating on her mouth, she felt weak in the knees. Although she wanted to deny it, desire was flooding her body. Blood rushed fast and furious through her veins. A hard thump pounded in her chest and a pool of heat gathered between her legs. The last thing she needed at that moment was all these sexual feelings, but they were there, complicating things.

He shifted his gaze lower, and, following the path of his gaze, she saw what now held his attention. Her nipples had hardened and were pressed against her blouse, making her arousal obvious.

His eyes returned to her mouth and he stood there for several moments before finally reaching out and placing his hands at her waist. The smile he gave her made her breath catch, and then he lowered his head and in one absolute imprisonment confined her lips to his.

She wound her arms around his neck. It was either that or slither to the floor from the impact of his kiss. The moment he captured her tongue, she was a goner. Then he released it, taking free rein of her mouth, unrestricted. She felt every touch, every flicker, every bold movement of his tongue—direct, unguarded, unrestrained.

A moan escaped from deep in her throat. She felt her resolve weakening when a scene of her in that bed across the room flashed through her mind. And he was there in that bed with her, hovering over her, making any resistance melt away.

A loud bang below had her jumping back out of his arms, drawing in a deep breath. She suppressed an inner shiver when she met his heated gaze, and she knew if given the chance he would pull her back in his arms and kiss her again, even take it to another level. Lord help her, but she needed to get out of there.

"I need to leave. Now," she said in a strained voice.

As if he understood, he nodded. "All right."

Taking her hand in his, he led her out of the room and toward the elevator. Lucky for her the doors opened the moment he pressed the button, and she quickly stepped inside.

When she saw he was about to join her, she said quickly, "You don't have to ride down with me."

The smile he gave her made her breath catch. "I know, but I wouldn't have it any other way. Regardless of what you might think, I can be a gentleman," he said, pushing a button for the lower floor.

Instead of speaking, she just nodded. She would be sure to add *gentleman* beneath *good kisser* on her list of his many attributes. Though she tried to ignore him once the elevator closed, he stood against the wall staring at her like he wanted to cross the space separating them and devour her.

She released a deep breath when the elevator stopped and the door swooshed open. She quickly stepped out and headed for the exit door. It was then that she heard the music. The band had started playing and the slow tune they were performing was one of her favorites. She unconsciously slowed her pace.

"Let's have at least one dance before you leave," Terrence whispered close to her ear as he took her hand in his.

She nodded, and within seconds he led her toward the dance floor. Heat surged through her the moment he pulled her into his arms. A frisson of sensual awareness invaded her entire being and the air surrounding them seemed supercharged. As if they had a mind of their own, her arms wrapped around him the same way his embraced her. She closed her eyes and placed her head on his chest despite thinking that she really needed to leave, go back to the safety of her home, and that dancing with him this way was too risky. But then, being held in his arms felt good, and like always when they were this close, she could feel her body responding to the pure masculinity of him. His muscles felt hard and firm beneath her fingers and she felt herself pressed even more tightly against him. Then her mind began wondering again.

She wondered how it would feel to have his skin beneath her fingertips, how the texture of it would taste on her tongue.

"Sherri."

It took her a full minute to realize he had called her name. She looked up into the darkness of his eyes, desire lining his pupils. "Yes?"

"I was dead serious when I invited you to spend the night," he leaned down and whispered huskily.

She considered his invitation, really considered it. Although it had been a long time since she'd been involved in a physical relationship with a man, she still wasn't ready to give herself to him so fully and completely. Because of Ben, she was going out of her way to safeguard her heart from further hurt and pain, and she believed an affair with Terrence would lead to just that.

The song had ended, but they were still standing in the middle of the dance floor. "Come, let's sit over here," he said, leading her to one of the tables near the windows.

"We want the same thing, Sherri," he said when they were seated. "I think you know that."

She glanced over at him. "I want more from a relationship than just the physical. I'll never settle for just that again, Terrence."

He nodded. "And a physical relationship is all I can ever offer a woman."

Sherri stared at him for a few moments before slowly standing. Her words held finality when she spoke. "Then it would never work between us, because we want different things." She sighed deeply. "I'm leaving, since we fully understand each other."

And then she headed for the exit door without looking back.

Chapter 4

"This is the Holy Terror, and you're tuned to WLCK, the Keys' most important stroke on your radio. Although some of you die-hard football fans want to get a head start discussing the coming season, today on *Sports Talk* we're talking about Wimbledon, the oldest tennis tournament in the world, which starts shortly. There're many tennis fans out there in the audience, and I want to hear from you."

Sherri stood in the glass-enclosed booth next to where Terrence sat with a computer monitor flashing in front of him. Mark, the person who was usually available to screen incoming calls for *Sports Talk*, had called in sick and with a limited staff working during the summer months, she'd pitched in to help, which would have been fine if it hadn't put her in close contact with Terrence.

It had been almost two weeks since that night he had invited her to dinner. Two solid weeks during which time they'd passed each other in the halls and sat across from each other in meetings while trying to ignore the sexual tension radiating between them. Sexual tension that her parting words to him hadn't been able to eradicate.

Sighing deeply, she checked the clock in the hall. Terrence's show lasted an hour, and it had just started. Even separated from him in the booth, she felt the effect of him just by listening to his voice. He had what most in the industry would refer to as a stroking voice, one that could pull a listener in.

He had gone into advertisements, giving five minutes before he was ready to take the first call.

As if he knew she was in the booth, he turned off his mike, took off his headset and looked her way. Their gazes locked. She felt the sensations she'd been trying to ignore, sensations she'd convinced herself had actually been a figment of her imagination. At this very moment he was proving her wrong. He was also making her remember that night the two of them had shared dinner alone. The kisses. Their dance. For her the Holy Terror experience was coming back in full force.

Her lips tightened when he leaned back in his chair and continued to study her. He should be keeping an eye on that computer monitor instead of on her. Likewise, she should be screening his incoming calls. She tried to ignore him but felt his gaze still glued to her, like that of a hungry predator with its next meal in focus.

Her only saving grace was that the jingle was about to end. She watched as he sat up straight in his chair, put his headset back on and turned the mike back on. Only then did he shift his attention from her.

She released a deep sigh. It was destined to be a long hour.

"Hi, Holy Terror, this is Monica."

Terrence couldn't help but smile. Monica Kendricks was a frequent caller no matter what sport they were discussing. And she was a notorious flirt. "Monica, what can I do for you today?"

"Several things," she said in that feminine chuckle that actually had the tendency to grate on his nerves. "But the one I'm safe in requesting of you is for you to end a disagreement between me and several of my girlfriends. They say the nineteen courts at Wimbledon are composed of just rye grass but I remember reading somewhere it was Bermuda grass."

The first thing that came into Terrence's mind was who gave a crap. Were there really women somewhere who'd been arguing about the type of grass on the courts at Wimbledon? He shook his head. "I hate to tell you this, Monica, but you lose. All the courts at Wimbledon are composed of rye grass." And before she could comment, he moved to the next call.

"This is the Holy Terror."

"Holy, this is Thomas."

"Yes, Thomas. What's your question?"

"It's about Serena and Venus."

"What about them?"

"Rumor has it you use to date one of them," Thomas said.

"And if I did?"

"Will you be joining one or both in London later this month?"

"No, sorry to disappoint you," Terrence said, smiling.

"Hey, you could never disappoint me, man. I was

there that night when the Dolphins clobbered the Cowboys to go to the Super Bowl thanks to your winning touchdown. You're the greatest."

He chuckled. "No, Muhammad Ali is."

"Oh, then you're the second greatest, and if you did date one of the Williams girls, then you're also my hero."

Terrence shook his head again. It was one of those days.

An hour later Terrence turned off his mike and removed his headset again before standing to work the kinks out of his body. He had gotten a record number of calls today. It seemed everyone had to say something about the Grand Slam season.

He glanced over at the glass booth. He could see the top of Sherri's head, which meant she was still there, probably telling disappointed callers the show was over. His lips curved into a smile when she stood and caught his eye. They hadn't said a word to each other for a couple of weeks while effectively waging one hell of a mental battle. As far as he was concerned such a battle could be fought anywhere but could only end in the bedroom.

Okay, so they were at opposing crossroads. She had happily ever after in her sights and he had no plans of indulging in anything remotely close. But what did that have to do with overactive testosterone and raging hormones? They were adults. They had needs. Who said they couldn't enjoy each other without any promises of tomorrow? No expectations. No obligations.

He imagined she assumed that she'd had the last word, and for the past couple of weeks he'd let her. That had given him time to think, make a few decisions and formulate a revised plan. The bottom line was that, for a reason he still hadn't yet figured out, he wanted her. He'd wanted other women in the past, but none with this degree of wanting. It kept him up at night with thoughts of how it would feel to slide between those luscious-looking thighs.

The two kisses they'd shared that night had done more damage than good. He thought if the kisses alone were that explosive, how would it feel to get naked with her, share her bed, get inside her body and take the word *stroking* to a whole other level and then some? He got hard just thinking about it. With him, being hard equated to one thing: getting laid.

Playing Mr. Nice with her hadn't gotten him anywhere, so it was time he lived up to his name. Determined, he moved toward the booth at the same time she came out of it. He stopped dead in his tracks wondering how a woman could look both professional and sexy at the same time. She liked wearing those business suits, and one of these days he intended to peel one right off her body, along with whatever she was wearing underneath.

He began walking again and came to a stop in front of her. He felt the sexual tension, a lot stronger today. "Hello, Sherri."

"Terrence. It was a nice show."

He smiled. "Thanks. And you look nice."

He hated making small talk when what he really wanted to do was scoop her up into his arms and take her somewhere—her office was one consideration—and make love to her until she begged for more and then start the hot and delicious process all over again until they were out of each other's systems.

"Thank you."

"So what are you doing for lunch?" he asked, looking at his watch.

"Haven't made any plans yet," she responded softly. "More than likely I'll work through lunch."

He looked back at her and smiled. "And miss the opportunity of going off somewhere with me to make out?"

Any doubts he'd had that she wanted him as much as he wanted her dissolved then and there. Desire was there in the eyes looking back at him. It was there in her expression, although she was trying like hell to hide it. Why was she so opposed to a short, no-strings-attached affair? Why couldn't she forget about that jerk who evidently hadn't appreciated her? And couldn't she temporarily suspend the idea of a little house and white picket fence? That could come later with some nice, willing guy who shared her views on the whole forever-after thing. What she and he needed to concentrate on was the needless torture they were going through now.

"How many times do I have to tell you that an affair between us won't work, Terrence?" she said with impatience in her voice.

"As many times as I'm going to tell you that it will not only work but it's a necessity."

She rolled her eyes. "A necessity? That's a good one." Her lips twitched in a smirk.

Now he was the impatient one. "Don't let me wipe that smirk off your face in a way that will have you moaning my name, Sherri."

Her smirk immediately turned to a frown. "I think you've said enough. My uncle may have given you free rein to say or do what you please around here, but I'm not included on your agenda."

He moved a step closer. "Baby, starting today you

are my agenda," he said, his voice a low rumble. "Don't confuse the Mr. Nice and Persistent guy from before. Now all is fair in love and war."

She lifted her chin and glared at him. "Oh, now are you saying you're capable of falling in love?"

Now it was his turn to frown. "No, what I'm saying is not even close. But actions will speak louder than words. You'll see what I mean."

"I'm opposed to whatever you're thinking of doing."

A mischievous smile touched his lips. "Okay, I'll keep that in mind."

She inhaled deeply. "You really don't get it, do you?"

He chuckled. "Yeah, it's kind of hard for me to get it when you're emitting such hot vibes whether you want to send them or not. Now I'm giving you fair warning that I plan to act on them. And trust me when I say that you'll be the one *getting* it. Now if you will excuse me I need to go check on things at the club. You're welcome to join me for dinner if you like."

"No, thank you," she said firmly.

He smiled. "If you change your mind, just show up. I like surprises."

"He likes surprises. The nerve of the man!" Sherri muttered under her breath as she made her way back to her office. She had a good mind to turn around and tell him just where he could stick those surprises he liked so much.

Her footsteps halted when she saw her uncle walking quickly toward her office. "Uncle Warrick, you need to see me?"

"Yes, I just got a call from Jeremy Wilkins. He's decided to sell WSOV after all and wants to give me first dibs."

Sherri couldn't help but smile. "Uncle Warrick, that's wonderful. I know how long you've wanted to operate a station in Memphis."

"Yes, well, keep your fingers crossed that the negotiations are successful. Wilkins can be hard as nails at times, and he knows how much I want that station. The worst thing you can ever do is to let your opponent know how anxious you are to get something."

Evidently nobody ever told that to Terrence, she thought. "How soon will you be leaving?"

"Just as soon as I can get to the airport," he said as they walked toward her office. "Wilkins has sent his private jet for me. I put my feelers out, and from what I hear he's in a little financial bind. He might know I want to buy the station, but it helps me to know just how much he needs to sell it."

Sherri admired her uncle. His goal had been to

own at least five radio stations before he turned forty, which he'd done. Now, at fifty-five, he owned fifteen across the country.

"That means I'm leaving you completely in charge while I'm gone," he said as they entered her office. "It might take me a full week to work out all the details and return as owner of station number sixteen."

Her uncle's excitement was contagious. "Don't worry about a thing while you're away. I'll handle everything and everyone."

His brow raised. "What about the Holy Terror? Have the two of you been getting along any better than the last time we talked?"

With her hand, she waved aside any of her uncle's concerns. "Everything's fine," she lied. "Terrence and I understand each other," she added, wishing that were true. She and Terrence did not understand each other. After two weeks of good behavior he was back to being difficult.

Her uncle studied her. "Are you sure? Because if not, I can talk with him." He smiled. "I think he makes a pest of himself with you because he likes you."

Sherri had to refrain from telling her uncle that Terrence didn't like her, he *wanted* her. There was a difference. "I doubt that's true, but like I said, Terrence and I understand each other. Don't worry about anything back here. Just go on to Memphis and work out a good deal with Wilkins. I'll take care of everything while you're gone."

Chapter 5

Just when she'd thought her and Terrence's paths wouldn't be crossing any more that week, she ran into him, of all places, on the elevator. And to make matters worse, he was the lone occupant.

"Going down, Sherri?" he asked, his voice lowering to too husky a pitch for her peace of mind. And it didn't help the situation to know that for some reason he had invaded her dreams last night in ways he hadn't invaded them before. They had been sexy. Naughty. And in her dreams he had been the one going down. The memory of it had the insides of her thighs feeling damp. Now there he stood, leaning against the wall and looking sexy as all outdoors.

"Yes." She hesitated a moment before stepping in and moving to one side, a safe distance away from him. The man was way too much temptation.

"Don't think you can control yourself in here alone with me?" he asked in a teasing voice.

"I'm the one who should be asking you that," she said, snapping out the words. Too late, she wished she hadn't when she saw the darkening of his eyes. The look he was giving her had the pulse beating erratically at the base of her throat.

"Since you brought it up," he said, his gaze roaming her figure from head to toe, "I was going to be a gentleman and control myself, but now I don't think I will."

She backed up and lifted her chin. "You will force me to do something against my will?" she asked.

He smiled that sexy smile of his and she knew she'd lost the battle already. That darn dimple did her in. "No, but I may force you to admit something you're being rather stubborn about. Although our relationship goals in life are different right now, this very moment in time, we want each other and there is no way you can deny it."

"I do deny it."

"Let's see for how long."

He moved away from the wall and reached out and pushed the button to stop the elevator. Then he took the few steps separating them. She refused to back up, determined to hold her ground with him.

"I need this kiss, Sherri, so if nothing else, please humor me," he murmured in a low voice.

The words he'd spoken had come as a surprise, and despite her reason for not wanting it to happen, she inwardly admitted that she needed the kiss, as well. So she did what he asked and humored him, although when his mouth settled on hers it was obvious neither of them was amused. Instead they were filled with one gigantic need.

Judging by the depth of their kiss, it was a need they were determined to fill. Just like the two other times their mouths had been joined, what they were experiencing was ultimate pleasure. The kind that slaughtered your senses, sent shudders through your body. As if they had a will of their own, their bodies pressed closer together in a way that bordered on indecent.

Sherri's purse fell to the floor when she wrapped her arms around Terrence's neck and sank even deeper into the kiss. She felt heated sensations all the way to her toes. This was the reason she'd tried to resist him. He had a way of making her not think straight. The last thing she should be doing with him was locking lips, getting some tongue play.

Yet that was exactly what she wanted to do—and she was enjoying every minute of it.

When he pulled his mouth away, she nearly moaned in protest. But he didn't move his mouth far. His tongue played around the corners of her lips. His actions ripped into what little control she had left. She felt overwhelmed by desire.

"Tell me I can come over tonight, Sherri. Let's finish up what we started here," he whispered against her moist lips.

She was tempted to concede. He was stirring up emotions within her that she'd never had to deal with before. The only excuse she could come up with was that her hormones were obviously out of whack. How long had it been since she'd been intimate with a man? Two years? Probably longer than that given the fact that she and Ben had never made love on a frequent basis. Whenever they could fit it into their schedules had worked well for them…or so she had thought. She'd found out later he'd been making love to someone else, a woman who worked for him. Someone who had no qualms about banging her way to the top. Sherri drew in a deep breath, not wanting to think about Ben's betrayal.

"We've held this elevator up long enough. Time to get out of here," Terrence said, breaking into her thoughts and taking her by the hand.

As soon as the elevator door opened, he stepped out and tugged her with him. Luckily they were in the parking garage, because he then pulled her into his arms and kissed her again. Sherri felt weak in the knees and felt blood rush to her head with every precise stroke of his tongue.

When he pulled back, she held on to him because it seemed the world around her was spinning. "Do I get to follow you home and spend some time with you?" he asked.

She looked at him, making a quick decision. She had tried to avoid him for two weeks and look what happened. Now she was behaving like a woman in heat. She needed to do whatever it took to get him out of her system, and if spending one night with him was the answer, then she would go through with it. Terrence had an allure she could not resist. At least not tonight.

"I need to think about it," she said softly.

He nodded. "Promise me you'll give it a lot of thought."

She stared up at him, becoming hypnotized by the eyes staring back at her. Deep. Dark. Hungry. He wanted her. There was no doubt in her mind. And she wanted him, but she had never been a person to engage in casual affairs. After her fiasco with Ben, maybe it was time to grab what she could and not believe in the forever after.

There was something about Terrence, the way he looked at her, the arrogant way he acted around her. In a way, she liked his arrogance. He was a self-assured man. Confident. A man who was persistent in going after what he wanted.

"I promise," she said softly, not sure what was happening to her to even consider such a thing.

A struggle was taking place within her, and she wasn't sure of the outcome. The only thing she did know was that since day one she had fought her feelings, tried to ignore her desires for Terrence, and it wasn't working. She hated to admit it, but he had been a part of her every thought even when she hadn't wanted him to be. Evidently he felt being smooth and debonair didn't work with her and was now behaving like a bad boy. She'd never messed with bad boys before. All the guys she'd dated in the past, even Ben, had gotten a stamp of approval from her parents.

"If you make a decision in my favor, I'll be at home tonight. I won't be at Club Hurricane," he said, breaking into her thoughts.

She doubted she would make a decision about anything tonight. She knew that any affair with Terrence, even a one-night stand, was destined to change her life forever. He was determined to set fire to a passion within her that had been left dormant for the past two years. Her nerve endings tingled at the thought of that happening.

"I've got to go," she said, moving away toward her parked car.

"All right. And I hope to see you later. You do have my address, right?"

She nodded. Although she'd never been to his home, she knew his address. It was within a mile of where she was currently living. "Yes."

And then she walked away and forced herself not to look back.

Feeling a sense of impending doom, Terrence stood with his hands deep in his pockets and watched Sherri walk away. Never had any woman's decision meant so much to him that it had his stomach tied in knots. From the beginning he'd thought that he was the one calling the shots.

Now he wasn't so damn sure of that.

When he'd first seen her he had quickly decided she was someone worth looking at, and there was no harm in looking. Once he'd discovered she was Warrick's niece, any thoughts of hitting on her vanished, although he'd seen no harm in a little innocent flirtation. But then he discovered looking and flirting weren't good enough. He wanted to touch and taste her, to join their bodies together. The more he'd seen her, the more he had wanted her. Now he was driven with an impulse to strip her naked each and every time he saw her.

She affected him like no other woman had. For two weeks they had tried avoiding each other and he'd been fine with it, deciding a woman with marriage on her mind was the last type of woman he needed to get involved with. Yet the moment he had glanced at the glass booth and seen her in it, it was as if a part of her had called out to him, had made his desire for her keener, his obsession with sharing a bed with her even more defined.

He stood there and continued to watch as the car she'd gotten into drove off and disappeared. Now the waiting would begin. Taking his hands out of his pockets, he walked toward his car, thinking he needed to make love to her like he needed to breathe.

For him to want any woman that much wasn't good. But for the time being, he was trapped by his desires and only she held the key for his release.

* * *

Sherri walked into the house, thinking that during the drive home her head should have cleared and her senses should have been back in check. But if that was the case, then why was she contemplating taking a shower, changing into something sexy and paying Terrence a visit?

And why on the drive home had she felt the need to constantly remind herself that she was a forever-after kind of girl, and just because Ben hadn't appreciated her that didn't necessarily mean the next guy wouldn't? On top of all that, she also reminded herself she didn't have the time to put into an affair, long or short. Her concentration was on her work at the station. She felt good knowing her uncle believed in her capabilities enough to leave her in charge of everything and everyone.

Including Terrence.

But only technically, since being in charge of the station included responsibility for anyone associated with it.

She moved through her living room and headed straight for the kitchen, needing a cup of tea. She always thought better while sipping tea.

A short while later she was sitting at the kitchen table sipping tea and trying to decide what she should do. Why would a logical person like herself even contemplate doing something so illogical as having an affair, and with of all people, the Keys' bad boy? A man with a reputation as a ladies' man. A man who never, ever intended to marry. What was the sense in that? She took a sip of her tea and summed up the answer in five words.

She needed a memorable experience.

She was twenty-seven and had yet to experience the big O. At least not a real one. She hadn't ever told anyone, including Kim, that her time in bed with Ben had always left her so unsatisfied that she had begun wondering what all the hoopla was about regarding sex. Though Ben had never complained and had in fact several times complimented her on the degree of passion she could generate in their bed, she'd always inwardly felt shortchanged. She smiled, thinking that she would love to see Ben now and confess that all those times she'd actually been faking it.

Her smile quickly vanished when another thought crossed her mind. What if Ben had been faking it, as well? What if the reason he had left her for another woman had nothing to do with her spending more time on the job than with him? What if that had only been his excuse for her replacement?

She took another sip of tea and thought about all those possibilities. A short while later she knew she had to know the truth. Could she satisfy a man in bed? Could a man satisfy her? She nervously placed her cup back down in the saucer. Maybe she was thinking too hard. She'd never underestimated herself as a woman. She was healthy, in good shape, dressed nicely. Men looked at her, Terrence wanted her. But all they saw was the book's cover. What was really on the pages? What if she wasn't capable of delivering when a man needed it the most?

She had to know the truth.

Convincing herself that she was doing this more for herself than for Terrence, she made her decision. One night with Terrence ought to give her the answer she wanted. One night and not any more and she would make certain he understood that. To make absolutely sure she wouldn't be another notch on his bedpost, she went to get her cell phone from out of her purse.

She called Terrence. He answered on the first ring. "Hello, Sherri."

She frowned. At times she detested caller ID. "Hello, Terrence. I've decided not to come over to your place. But you're more than welcome if you'd like to come over to mine."

He didn't say anything for a second, and then, "I'd love to."

"And, Terrence, just to make sure things are absolutely clear, tonight is the only night you'll get invited to my home. There will only be tonight for us. There will not be any repeats."

Again he didn't say anything for a second, and then, "I'll be there shortly."

Sherri hung up the phone. She refused to be just another notch on his bedpost, but he could definitely be a notch on hers.

Chapter 6

By the time Sherri had showered and changed into something more comfortable, Terrence was ringing the doorbell. Although her outfit, a printed skirt and blouse lounging set, was supposed to be relaxing, she found that she was a nervous wreck.

Twice she was tempted to call Terrence and tell him that she had changed her mind, but each time she decided to go through with it. She deserved to know the truth about herself.

Taking a deep breath, she opened the door. He stood there, not surprisingly looking positively jaw-droppingly sexy. The man was as macho as they came. He had changed out of the outfit he'd had on at the station and was dressed in a pair of jeans and a pullover. His hair appeared damp, which meant he'd showered and shaved.

"Terrence, welcome to my home," she said, attempting to add a degree of warmth and hospitality to her smile. "Won't you come in?"

"Yes, I definitely want to come in," he assured her, stepping over the threshold when she moved aside.

When she closed the door and turned, he was standing in the middle of her apartment and glancing around. "Nice place, Sherri. It suits you."

She chuckled, not sure what he meant by that. "Thanks." She gestured toward the sofa. "Please have a seat. Would you like anything to drink?"

"No thanks, I'm fine," he said, sitting down.

"All right, then I'll get dinner—"

"Dinner?"

She saw the surprised expression in his eyes and understood. Evidently he'd assumed that he would be escorted immediately to the bedroom. "Yes, dinner. After the wonderful meal you had prepared for me at the club, there was no way I could invite you over and not return the hospitality. Although I didn't have time to prepare anything, so I ordered from a nice Chinese restaurant around the corner. I understand you like Chinese food."

"And who told you that?" he asked, looking at her intently.

"Um, I think I overheard one of the technicians mention it one day during lunch. So do you enjoy Chinese food?"

He leaned back in his seat. "Yes, I enjoy a number of things and Chinese food happens to be on the list."

"Good. It will only take me a second to set things up." She turned toward the kitchen.

"Sherri?"

She turned back around. "Yes?"

He met her gaze, and she could tell from the look in his eyes that he definitely had an agenda. He confirmed it when he asked, "Dinner isn't the only thing I'm getting tonight, right?"

Her reaction to his bold question was instantaneous. Her nipples hardened and heat began forming between her thighs. "Why? Is there something else that you want?" she asked, trying to keep her body from quivering.

He smiled, and her gaze shifted from his eyes to his mouth. She immediately recalled the kisses they'd shared, and just thinking about the intensity of them had goose bumps forming on her arms.

"Yes, there's something else I want. Do you want me to tell you what it is?"

She swallowed deeply. Not at any time did she doubt that he would. "I don't think that will be necessary, and as far as what else you'll be getting tonight, we will have to see. Some things are better when they are not planned or expected."

He shook his head. "I happen to disagree. I have nothing against spontaneity, but it's nice to know what's in store. Accidents can happen when things aren't planned or expected."

She nodded, catching his drift. But in this case, as he would find out later, he had nothing to worry about since she was in good health and on the pill. "True, but a smart man and woman are always prepared regardless."

Deciding not to say anything else on the subject, she moved toward the kitchen.

Terrence watched Sherri walk away. He was definitely prepared, since he'd put several condoms in his wallet. And just in case they decided to make it an all-nighter, he'd put a few in his jeans pockets, too. To be quite honest, although he'd hoped that she would, he'd been sort of surprised that she had called him. He wasn't sure of the reason, but he was not about to complain.

He heard her moving around in the kitchen and decided to check out the various paintings on the wall. A friend once said you could tell a lot about a woman by the pictures on her walls. In that case, Sherri must love animals, because he noticed several framed portraits of them. And one could safely say she liked live plants, judging from the many she had. Obviously she did a good job keeping them alive. Too bad he couldn't say the same about himself.

"Dinner is ready."

He glanced over in her direction and every nerve ending in his body vibrated. He meant to tell her earlier how much he liked her outfit and how good she looked in it. This was only the second time he'd seen her dressed in anything other than a business suit, and he couldn't wait for later when he got to see her wearing nothing at all. Deciding the sooner they finished dinner the sooner they could move on to other things, he crossed the room to her.

"I hope you're hungry," she said.

He couldn't help but smile at that. He was hungry, and once he got a taste of what he *really* wanted, he planned to gobble it up. "Yes, I'm hungry."

And then, taking her by surprise, he leaned forward and captured her mouth with his, causing heat to immediately flare within him. And her. He felt it when he used his tongue to tangle with hers, stroking pleasure she probably didn't want to respond to. But she was doing so anyway.

He broke the kiss and pulled in a deep breath. Just that first sensuous vibration made his stomach tremble and tempted him to lean over and capture her mouth again. But he didn't.

"What was that for?" she asked in a low, stunned voice, searching his face and at the same time licking her lips.

He grinned. "I'd thought it was time to let you know that although you're providing dinner, I intend to serve the dessert."

He intended to serve dessert.

All Sherri could do was sit across from him at her dinner table and make an attempt to enjoy what was her favorite food—shrimp fried rice—while trying not to imagine what kind of dessert he would be serving. She had ideas, of course. And those ideas had heat settling between her legs.

"You okay?"

She quickly glanced over at Terrence. He was sipping his wine and looking at her. She wondered if he knew what she was thinking, and if so, if he was amused by it all. "I'm fine. Why do you ask?"

He smiled. "No reason, other than you've barely touched your food."

She glanced down at her plate. She had eaten enough. "I had a huge lunch today."

She glanced over at his plate. It was clean. "I take it that you were hungry."

He chuckled. "Yes, evidently. Well, at least since it was takeout, there're no dishes to wash. Saves time."

She met his gaze. Was getting her into bed all he could think about? From the look in his eyes, evidently so. She stood and began clearing off the table, and he automatically stood to assist. "You don't have to help," she said, hoping that he wouldn't.

"Why don't you go on into the living room and get comfortable," she suggested. "You might want to check out my selection of DVDs. There might be something you want to see."

"A movie?" he asked with the same surprise that he'd had when she'd mentioned dinner.

She couldn't help but smile. "Yes. It won't take me long to finish up in here."

He glanced at the table. "Are you sure you don't need my help?"

"I'm positive."

"Then I'll be waiting for you in the living room."

I just bet you will. As soon as he was gone, she let out a long breath. Anyone could tell she was out of her element with Terrence and serious doubt began to cloud her mind. What if the reason Ben had left her was because she'd been a disappointment to him? That meant chances were she probably wouldn't be able to satisfy Terrence, either. How would she handle seeing him around the station knowing she'd been a failure in bed?

She leaned against the kitchen counter. Why hadn't she thought this through before inviting him over? She knew the answer to that one. After that kiss in the elevator, she hadn't been thinking clearly.

By the time she'd finished wiping off the table, she was a nervous wreck and knew just what she had to do. Terrence was expecting a little hanky-panky tonight, and somehow she was going to get out of it. After placing the chairs back neatly under the table, she pulled in a deep breath before walking out of the kitchen.

It didn't take a rocket scientist to detect Sherri was nervous about tonight, and that was probably the reason she was stalling, Terrence thought while flipping through her collection of DVDs, none of which he cared to watch. None of them would be able to hold his attention. The only action he was interested in was the one that would take place in Sherri's bedroom.

If he thought he wanted her with a passion before, now his craving had doubled, possibly even tripled. It had been pure torture sitting across from her at the table while inhaling her scent, watching her eat and how, every so often, their gazes would meet in a heated clash. More than once he'd been tempted to push the food containers aside and have her then and there.

He needed to have tonight with her. Hopefully when it was over she would be out of his system, and his mind and body would go back to a normal state. He and Sherri understood what sharing a bed meant. Neither of them had any expectations beyond tonight.

"Terrence?"

He turned at the sound of her voice and once again he felt a tightening in his gut as he watched her cross the room to him. And when she came to a stop, it took all he had not to reach out and pull her into his arms and kiss her crazy. "Yes?"

"About tonight…" She was nervously twisting her fingers and her voice sounded unsteady.

He had an idea what she was going to say and knew immediately that he couldn't let her. They were too close to turn back now, and he needed to reassure her that things would be all right.

She opened her mouth to speak, but he quickly placed a finger to her lips. "Don't say it, Sherri. I feel your uncertainty about this, about us, but I want you to do something that you might find difficult to do."

He saw her throat tighten when she swallowed. "What?"

"Trust me enough to believe that in this situation, I know what we both need."

He watched as she studied his features and figured she was wondering how he could be so sure of what she needed. Inwardly, he was asking himself that same thing. It was scary, but he actually cared how she was feeling and he wasn't running a game on her just to get her in bed. He was being completely honest. For a reason he couldn't explain, one-night stand or not, he couldn't and wouldn't treat this affair like all his others. Although tonight would be all they had, it still meant a lot to him that she wanted things to happen as much as he did.

And he truly believed that she wanted him as much as he wanted her. He'd discovered that she had the ability to say one thing while meaning another, and as a man who was used to picking up vibes from women, he'd been able to home in on it. That was the reason he had been so persistent, working like hell to break through her resolve, wear down her resistance, so the two of them could have a night together they would both enjoy.

It was a gimme that he desired her more than any other woman, but there was something else between them, something he'd been trying to downplay, practically ignore. And it was something he wasn't capable of walking away from until she was out of his system. He needed tonight.

"Trust has to be earned, Terrence," she said softly, breaking into his thoughts.

"And I agree," he said, holding her gaze. His stomach clenched when she moistened her lips with the tip of her tongue. "Earning trust would be the normal course of action for most people, but we aren't most people, Sherri. I need you to trust me enough to believe this is the best course of action we can take to move on, to work each other out of our systems. This physical attraction has turned into a physical obsession, and there's only one way to end it. But I need you to feel safe with me."

Her lips tightened. "I do feel safe with you, Terrence, otherwise you wouldn't be here."

That's what he needed to hear. "Good." He reached out and took her hand. "Come here. Let's sit down and talk awhile."

Now it was her turn to look surprised. "Talk?"

He chuckled. "Yes, talk. And if we go beyond just talking, it will be left up to you."

She allowed him to lead her to the sofa, and when she moved to sit down beside him he pulled her into his lap. She started to get up, but his firm arms kept her immobile. "Stay still. I won't bite."

She parted her lips to say something, but then immediately closed them. Good thing. He would have been tempted to break his promise and make the first move by kissing her. He had such a weakness for her mouth, it was almost unnerving.

He shifted positions on the sofa, and once he had her tucked in his lap the way he wanted, he glanced down at her to find her staring at him. "Comfortable?"

"Yes."

"So," he said, trying to ignore the furious pounding of his heart, "what do you think of Key West so far?"

That question kicked off a series of others, sparking a lot of conversation between them, some of it serious, most not. His goal was to keep her talking so she could feel relaxed with him. And it was working. She sat up in his lap and shared with him how her cousins—Jackie, Reatha and Alyson—used to get into all kinds of trouble with their parents while growing up, and how Warrick was the one who would always come to their rescue. He could tell she was close to her uncle and sensed a special bond between them.

He couldn't help but study her while she talked. That she had loosened up was obvious in her face. No frowns. No scrunching up of her forehead. No glaring of the eyes. She had smooth skin, beautiful skin. And her eyes, ears and nose were perfect. Then there was her mouth. He quickly decided not to go there.

In good time the conversation switched to him, placing him in the spotlight. And he did something with her that he typically didn't do with other women. He shared a little about his pro career, his retirement from the game, his siblings, his father. He even went so far as to mention that his father was dating the woman who had been his secretary for over fifteen years. A woman everyone knew had been in love with him for years. He expressed just how happy he and his siblings were about the developing relationship and how they hoped to hear something of a planned wedding soon.

It was only after sharing that bit of news that he noticed just how cozy he and Sherri had gotten together. Sometime during the past hour or so, they had eased into a more comfortable spot on the sofa. He was reclining sideways with his back against the armrest and she was sprawled all over him. Only when there was a lag in conversation did either of them realize it. Sherri quickly made a move to sit up.

The hand he placed on her shoulder halted her. "Please stay."

She held his gaze for a long moment. Somewhere in her house he could actually hear the ticking of a clock, but for them it seemed time was standing still. That realization gaze him pause, and he continued to stare at her with the same intensity as she was staring at him. He became entranced, totally and irrevocably mesmerized, by the look in her eyes. In response, his body started getting hot; his desire was on the rise…as well as a certain part of his anatomy. The need to kiss her, touch her and play out his fantasies—the ones that invaded his nightly dreams—surged in him. But he fought back the temptation, determined to do what he'd promised and let her be in control. He had placed her in the driver's seat, and he was willing to go wherever she transported them.

"It's your call," he said in a deep, husky voice. "You can play or you can pass. Which do you want to do?"

She continued to hold his gaze, and then she closed her eyes for a brief moment. When she re-opened them, he immediately sensed a change in her and was well aware that she had made her decision. And by the look in her eyes, he had a gut feeling just what that decision would be. Yet his heart appeared to have stopped beating until she spoke aloud to confirm his assumption.

"I want to play."

He simply nodded as intense heat fired up his blood. After inhaling deeply, he said, "Your serve."

She slowly raised her body to lean forward, and he could feel the beating of her heart against his chest. Her hardened nipples felt right pressing into him, and her body's heat was combining with his, causing a frisson of electric energy. Never before had he wanted a woman more, and when she tilted her mouth upward toward his, he leaned in to meet her halfway.

Her mouth closed over his, and in that moment the full impact of what they were doing blasted through his loins and he felt his arousal pressed solidly against her thigh. If she minded the hard contact, she didn't show it. She was too busy tangling her tongue with his and stretching up as far as she could to take the kiss deeper and make it last longer.

He grabbed her around her waist and gently pulled her body closer. With a compulsive need, he deepened the kiss like it was the greatest gift he could ever receive. Something he had been waiting his lifetime to have.

What made it even more special was that she had been the one to initiate it. She was surrendering herself to him willingly, and he was taking her mouth greedily. He had been right all along: she was a very passionate woman. He could feel her passion, taste it. And more than anything, he wanted to bury himself in the very heat of that passion, right inside her.

When breathing became necessary, she pulled away from his mouth and leaned against the back of the sofa to breathe in deeply while staring into his face. Their positions had shifted again and somehow she had him on his back beneath her.

Her lips were swollen from their kiss, her eyes aflame with desire, her face flushed with sensual need. At that moment he realized that Sherri Griffin was no ordinary woman. No ordinary woman had the capability to do the things she was doing to him. She had his entire body throbbing, his blood rushing through his veins, his insides on fire.

"It's your turn," she said, severing his thoughts.

His breathing deepened to a feverish pitch. "Are you sure?"

He knew what giving him a turn meant, but he wanted to make sure she knew, as well. Before she could respond to his question, he said, "I think it's only fair to warn you that I've wanted you from that first day in Warrick's office. Since then I've dreamed about you and me together this way countless times. Fantasized about it, as well. Once I take my turn, Sherri, I might not be able to stop. Chances are that I won't."

To indicate that she fully understood, she nodded. And then she swallowed deep in her throat before asking in a breathless tone, "Do you intend to play or pass, Terrence?"

He shifted both their bodies sideways and then leaned in closer and said in a deep, husky voice, "I intend to play."

"Then it's your serve."

That was all he needed to hear.

Chapter 7

Terrence had kissed her several times before, but nothing, Sherri thought, could have prepared her for this. He wasn't just kissing her. He was staking a claim to her mouth that one would think went beyond a mere one-night stand. There was an urgent need within him. Demanding. And she felt it all the way through to her bones.

He was kissing her like she was the core to his very existence, and she could do nothing more than respond while her insides quivered and sensations surged through her nerve endings.

Then his hands seemed to roam everywhere, on

her breasts, underneath her skirt, touching her as if she belonged to him, not just for tonight but for days to come, weeks, months, years. The absurdity of that thought stuck in her mind, but not for long. The moment he used his legs to nudge her thighs apart and then put his hand between them to touch her intimately through her panties, any and all thoughts dispersed from her mind on a breathless moan. He pulled his hand back then and broke off their kiss, but she had a feeling he was just beginning.

And he proved her right.

Their eyes caught just seconds before he pushed back enough to start removing her clothes. He pulled her blouse easily over her head. Tossing it aside, he undid the front clasp of her bra in one smooth flick of the wrist. Once he had taken that off her, his gaze feasted on the twin globes and the hardened buds of her nipples. He sat back on his haunches, examined them in detail with his eyes, and she felt the heat of his gaze as it trailed all over her chest.

After getting his visual fill, he stood to remove her skirt. Words were not spoken between them. None were needed. It was accepted. Understood. She knew they wanted the same thing, and tonight they would be getting it.

With his fingers in the waistband of her skirt, he

gently eased it down her legs, baring all of her to him in the process. She was wearing a pair of bikini panties, but from the way he was looking at her she might as well not have been wearing anything at all.

The skirt went flying over the sofa, and she tilted her head back to look up at him. He smiled, and at that moment she was lost in a sea of desire so deep she felt herself drowning in it. But she knew there was no way he would let her go under. Tonight was far from over, and when he leaned down and picked her up in his arms, she knew it would be a long, hot night.

Following Sherri's direction, Terrence headed for her bedroom as a gigantic need roared to life inside him. It had been there all the time, increasing steadily in slow degrees, but now it seemed to have taken on a life of its own.

He placed her on the bed and then followed her, easing back into the soft bedcovers with her, craving the taste of her mouth again. Tangling with her tongue sent erotic sensations rushing down his veins, and when he finally pulled back from the kiss, he knew he would take pleasure in removing the last garment from her body.

Straddling her, he began easing her panties down

her legs. As soon as he tossed them aside, his gaze latched on to the area between her thighs. That part of her held his gaze tightly, and he seemed unable to release it. He finally shifted his eyes to roam over her entire body, and the only word that came to his mind was *beautiful.* Every delectable inch of her.

He stood and began removing his own clothes and couldn't get out of them fast enough. Seeing her in that bed naked and waiting for him was almost more than he could handle. He'd had more than his share of sexual encounters before, but none had him quivering from the inside out like this one.

He had taken off his shirt, but before he removed his jeans, he took out his wallet and retrieved the condom packs and tossed them on the bed. He pulled the others out of his back pocket.

She gave a little laugh. "So many?"

He undid his zipper. "Those are just a few. I have more in my car if we need them."

Her smile was replaced by supreme wonder. "You're kidding, right?"

He held her gaze. "No, I wouldn't kid you about something like that. Evidently you don't know how much I want you."

When he pushed his jeans down past his thighs, he saw her take in the size of him through his briefs.

She inhaled deeply before saying, "If I didn't before, I do now."

He smiled and when he kicked his jeans aside he knew he had to get inside her body fast. There was pleasure and then there was pleasure, and he had a feeling they would be experiencing it to the highest degree tonight.

He could barely remove his last stitch of clothing knowing her eyes were directly on him. Once he did and looked up, he saw that her eyes were glued to his aroused member, both amazement and uncertainty etched in her features.

After sheathing himself in a condom, he decided not to waste any more time. He strolled over to the bed and, lifting a knee onto it, reached out his hand. "Come here."

Unhesitatingly, she came to him, placing her hand in his and going willingly when he pulled her into his arms. She responded to him when he leaned in and closed his mouth over hers.

He slowly broke off the kiss and pulled back slightly. Meeting her gaze, he asked in a gruff voice, "Ready to play?"

The desire in her eyes deepened when she said, "Yes, I'm ready."

Satisfied with her response, he traced her heated

flesh from the pulse point in her neck to her breasts. When he touched the hardened tips, she sucked in a deep breath. He watched the play of emotions on her face and knew her breasts were a hot spot for her, one he would enjoy using to push her over the edge.

Now was as good a time as any.

Lowering his head, his tongue replaced his fingers and he greedily began devouring her nipples. They seemed ready for his mouth. Her moans were sensuous music to his ears. As his mouth had its way with her breasts, his hands joined in and cupped them, tenderly kneading the firm mounds.

And then his mouth moved lower and he felt her shudder, which only heightened his need, flamed his desire. When he got to her stomach, his tongue blazed a wet trail around her belly button before finally moving lower.

His hands closed over her thighs, held them immobile as he lowered his head to the apex where her feminine mound awaited. With a guttural moan, he dived in with a possessiveness that nearly drove him over the edge of sanity. He felt her response when he began tasting her with his tongue and now understood why he had wanted her so much. The primitive part of him was absorbed in her sensual scent, her delectable taste, in every single thing about her.

The lower part of his body began throbbing with the need to be joined with hers, and moments later he gave in to the need. He lifted his head, met her gaze and smiled before slowly easing his body upward over hers, sweeping her into his arms.

He needed to hold her, kiss her, share with her sensations that were affecting him through to his bones. And when he released her mouth he knew he had to love her in the most primitive way known to man.

For him it was no longer an option. It was a necessity.

His eyes held tightly to hers when he eased between her thighs and lifted her hips high in his hands. With the head of his hard and heated erection poised at the entry of her feminine mound, he nearly trembled in greed. His gaze remained focused on her, studying her eyes, scrutinizing her face. He wanted to see her reaction, needed to hear her response, at the exact moment his body entered hers. Why such a thing was so important to him, he wasn't sure. All he knew was that it was.

It was then that he decided to seize the moment, capitalize on the sensuous chemistry and sexual awareness surrounding them. His pulse was beating rapidly at the base of his throat, and his erection was throbbing hard in need. Slowly and with uninhibited deliberation, he pushed deep inside her, all the way to the hilt. Surprise then pleasure lit her features when her body accepted the full length and thickness of him. He heard her gasp, followed by a soft moan. Then he pulled out, just to thrust back into her again, watching her eyes dilate each time.

He held still for a second or else he would have exploded inside her, then and there. He needed to savor the moment, especially since this was the last time for both of them. He had to remember this was a one-night stand, but at that very moment, while on the brink of a sexual abyss, he didn't see how that could be. How in the world, after this, he could not come back for more. And more.

Something within him uncoiled and propelled him to move. Maybe it was those sexy sounds she was making, or the scent of their joining that was floating around them, over them, cloaking them in the potent aroma of a man and woman mating.

"Terrence!"

He held on to her, dragging in a deep breath when her feminine muscles clamped him tightly, squeezing and demanding the hot rush of his release. He gripped her hips and with one final thrust gave her what she wanted, what they both needed, and felt her come apart in his arms at the same moment he was ripped apart in hers. The same sensations that swept through him did likewise to her, rippling from head to toes.

His lips parted as he cried out her name, and when he felt his entire body get swept away, seemingly to the stars and beyond, he wondered if he would ever drift back down to earth again.

Sherri suddenly understood what it meant to be totally consumed in the art of making love. Terrence had taken her to a level of pleasure that she'd never traveled to before. The thought that this was what she should have been experiencing all those times she had been faking it hit a deep nerve. How was it possible for one man to so eloquently do what another one could not? How had Terrence given her the experience of a lifetime, her first big O, when Ben hadn't even come close?

She pulled in a deep breath, deciding not to think about it since it didn't matter any longer. Terrence had given her pleasure beyond measure, and from the way she saw things, she had pleased him, as well, which lifted a great burden off her shoulders. Nothing was wrong with her. She could be both the recipient and giver of pleasure.

Something else Terrence had shown her was the fact that she was capable of falling in love again, because as much as she didn't want it to happen, as much as she didn't need it to happen, she was afraid she could be falling in love with him. She inhaled deeply, thinking that he was the last person a sane woman would want to give her heart to.

"Sherri?"

She glanced up and met his gaze. He had slumped down beside her and was drawing in deep breaths of air. "Yes?"

"We're not through yet tonight. I gave you fair warning."

She nodded, remembering. He had. She felt his touch between her thighs and immediately her body responded. And then he was there, leaning up on his elbows, all in her face, about to get all in her mouth. And the only thing she could think of at that very moment was that she was ready, willing and able to go the next round with him. More than anything, she wanted to make love with him again. She would share her body with him, but she was determined to keep her heart under lock and key.

The opening and closing of the bathroom door jerked Terrence awake, made him recall just where he was and in whose bed he had spent the night. He glanced out the window. It was morning.

He stretched his body and then leaned up on his elbow to glance at the clock on Sherri's nightstand. It was just a little past seven. When he heard the sound of the shower going, he slumped back down beneath the covers. He was tempted to go join her but doubted he could move his body. To claim he was sensuously exhausted was an understatement.

Just how many times had they made love? How many orgasms had they shared? Hell, he wasn't sure. At some point he had stopped counting. Her need to mate had been just as fierce as his. Before last night he'd never had a reason to care about any woman's past relationships, but in Sherri's case he had a feeling her past lover hadn't been taking care of business properly. Some of the positions they'd tried had been new to her, but she hadn't hesitated to go for it, finding satisfaction and giving him his. He smiled when he remembered he had basically ridden her to sleep right after an orgasm had hit them both. He hadn't been able to stop his body from thrusting into her until he had nothing else to give. It had been only then that he had slumped down beside her and pulled her into his arms, where they both succumbed to blissful slumber.

He threw his hand over his eyes when something occurred to him. He had known making love to her would be powerful, but what he hadn't expected was for her to blow his mind in such a way that the very thought that this would never happen again between them was totally, absolutely unacceptable.

He inwardly groaned. When had the thought of leaving a woman's bed without looking back ever bothered him? Most of the time when the sex act was over, he was the first one gone. But not this time. He wondered how he could convince her that last night should be the beginning for them and not the end. And he knew why. The woman had gotten under his skin, and one night of lovemaking wouldn't be able to get her out.

He actually liked her. He liked her smile, which she was giving him more of these last couple of days, and he liked the way she looked at him when she thought he wasn't looking. He liked the way she made those little sounds right before she came and the way her body responded so quickly whenever he touched her.

Amazingly he was beginning to understand her, something he'd never taken the time to do with other women. He doubted she realized it, but when they had been holding their in-depth conversations, he had listened carefully and had heard everything she'd said and had picked up on a number of things she hadn't said. He couldn't help but admire a woman who knew what she wanted and worked hard to achieve it. She wanted to one day manage WLCK, and he could respect that and had no doubt she would achieve that goal.

But what he needed to show her was that she could have the best of both worlds. A career and a man. From the information he'd been able to weasel out of Warrick, her fiancé had broken their engagement, claiming she had made her desire for a career more important than her desire for him. Meanwhile he'd sought the attention of another woman. Jeez. What kind of ass reason was that to cheat? Even he was smart enough to know it was the quality and not the quantity of time that mattered in a relationship. His father had proven that when he had juggled being a single father and an attorney. Evidently no one had explained it to Sherri's boyfriend.

He glanced at her nightstand and saw all the empty condom packs there. They sure had gone through plenty, but there was more where those came from. The last thing he wanted was to get any woman pregnant. He closed his eyes, and in the outer reaches of his mind he saw Sherri. She was standing at the window in his club, and she smiled at him. When he glanced down the full length of her body, he saw she was pregnant, with his child. His hand went out to touch her stomach, to feel the movement of his—

He forced his eyes back open. How could he possibly imagine something like that? Why would he imagine something like that? He'd sworn never to be a husband or a father, so why had such thoughts entered his mind?

When the answers came, they hit him as one sharp kick in his gut. For the first time in his life, he had fallen for a woman. That was why he had been pursuing her like an obsessed moron this past month. But for some reason he wasn't thrown into an extreme panic attack as he should have been.

Nor was he in a state of denial.

He turned over in bed and smothered his head in the pillow, immediately picking up her scent. And then his mind became filled with memories of last night, and he couldn't think of a better way to start off the day. With that thought deeply entrenched in his mind, he got out of the bed.

The warm water flowing down on her made Sherri realize just how sensitive certain areas of her body were. When she glanced down and saw all the marks of passion practically everywhere, she couldn't help but recall the intensity of her and Terrence's lovemaking.

The man had given her what no other man had—her first sampling of sexual fulfillment. And it had been good. Over-the-top. For the past month he had made it blatantly clear that he wanted her. And last night, when he'd finally gotten her, he had delivered big-time. He had been capable of stroking desires she hadn't known she had. She hadn't just managed a single orgasm; on more than one occasion, he had driven her to multiples.

The man was a sexual sensation on legs. Where did he get his energy? His staying power? His ability to make her scream to the point where her throat felt sore? And he was still there in her bed. At least that was where she had left him. She was surprised he was still there when she had awakened. From what she'd heard, he was good at making quick escapes the morning after.

If he had decided to sneak out while she was in the shower, she would hope that he remembered their agreement—not that she thought he would forget. Men like Terrence wouldn't forget. Last night might have held a lot of revelations and satisfaction for her, but it meant nothing to him other than finally scoring. He would move on. It was expected.

In a way she was glad he had that attitude since

that made it easier for her to scoff at the idea, the mere possibility, that she was falling in love with him. She didn't want to become involved with a man no matter how good he was in bed. She reminded herself that the only thing she had time to concentrate on was achieving her goals.

She had made love enough times with Terrence last night to last a lifetime. Somewhere out there was a man who would love and cherish her, but she didn't want him to find her any time soon. Working on a relationship took up too much time, time she didn't have to spare. Although she still resented the way and the reason Ben had left, his leaving had in truth been a blessing. He would never have agreed to quit his job with that prestigious law firm in Cleveland to move to the Keys. He would have flatly refused, and she would have given up the chance to pursue the dream of a lifetime.

"Mind if I join you?"

She jerked around so fast she almost slipped and would have done so if a naked Terrence hadn't reached out to steady her. "W-what are you doing here?" she asked.

"I spent the night here, remember?" he said, smiling as he reached out to grab the soap out of the dish behind her.

She stood there, speechless, and watched as he rubbed the soap—*her* soap—over his chest and stomach before moving down his thighs and legs, working up a lathery foam. She tried to downplay the sensations settling between her legs as she stood there staring.

"You do remember that I spent the night," he said, in an attempt to get her attention again.

She dragged her gaze back to his face. "Yes, but I assumed you would be gone when I got out of the shower."

"What would make you think such a thing?" he asked as he continued to scrub soap all over his body. "And do you mind stepping aside for a moment? You're blocking the flow of water."

And getting drenched in the process, she thought, glaring at him as she did as he requested and moved aside. It was a good thing her shower stall was big enough for two. "The reason I thought such a thing," she said, trying to ignore the way the water was washing away the soap foam from his body, "is because it's my understanding—through the rumor mill—that that's how you operate."

Using his hand, he wiped water off his face and smiled over at her. "You've been checking up on my techniques? That's cute. You really didn't have to waste your time doing that. If there was something you needed to know, all you had to do was ask."

She narrowed her gaze at him. "I wasn't interested. It was merely watercooler gossip that I overheard."

He lifted a brow. "That's strange since until last night I hadn't slept with anyone at the station for them to know what I do or don't do."

"Doesn't matter. Apparently they were wrong."

"Technically they were right. I usually don't hang around."

Sherri frowned in confusion. "In that case, why are you here?"

He smiled, and before she could blink he had backed her up against the wall and simultaneously lifted her legs around his waist. "For this."

And then he was kissing her, stoking the same fires within her that he had flaming out of control last night. Her nipples ached and the apex of her thighs throbbed, but she forgot everything the moment his tongue entered her mouth. Then she was helpless to do anything but kiss him back…not that she had any qualms about doing so.

It didn't take long for her entire body to respond. When he spread her legs apart and drove into her, she literally screamed out loud from the pleasure he evoked. Pleasure that overwhelmed her senses and racked her mind. She looked up into his eyes and understood at that moment that he was teetering as close to the edge as she was. And then she remembered one vital thing. He wasn't wearing a condom. What had he said last night? *Accidents can happen when things aren't planned or expected.*

She was on the pill, so she wasn't worried. Still, she would definitely remind him of that statement. Later. Not now. The only thing she wanted to think about now was the way he was making her feel. Like a woman being smothered in bliss and making up for lost time.

Her heels dug into his back with each one of his powerful thrusts into her body. Moments later, when passion overtook them, she felt herself shattering in a million pieces. He broke off the kiss and let out a deep, hard groan the same time she screamed his name. Together they were propelled to a higher plane and reached the pinnacle of sexual gratification.

"You forgot to use a condom when we were in the shower."

Terrence swore and stopped short as they walked out her front door. Forgetting something that important had never happened to him before. Never. That just showed how much the woman affected him. He'd envisioned her pregnant in his mind and had done the unthinkable by risking the chance of it becoming a reality. "It wasn't intentional and I apologize," he said. "I'm more responsible than that. I take full responsibility if you—"

"Relax," Sherri said, giving him a wry smile. "I'm on the pill. I just wanted to remind you of what you said last night. Besides, you did bring enough condoms with you. It just slipped your mind. Things like that can happen."

He was grateful for her understanding. "Yes, but if for some reason the pill doesn't work, then I—"

"You'll be the first to know," she said, smiling.

"Would you like to go with me to the club for breakfast?"

She glanced at her watch. "I have to fill in for Uncle Warrick at an off-site meeting this morning."

"Perhaps another time, then."

She didn't say anything for a minute, but when they reached her car, she said, "Thanks for last night, Terrence. It was special. I will remember it for a long time."

He didn't say anything for a minute, and then, "Would you be willing to do it again sometime? Sometime soon, like tonight?"

He could tell his question took her by surprise. "Why would we want to?"

He chuckled. "You can ask me that after last night, Sherri? We're good together. We both enjoyed it. You're not serious about anyone, and neither am I."

She narrowed her eyes at him. "I believe we covered all of that before and it was decided that we don't want the same thing in life. You just want a physical relationship, and I want something more. At least eventually. A smart woman would never let herself fall in love with you, because it would be a love that led nowhere."

He stared at her for a second. The latter part of what she'd said was true, at least that had been the story of his life until he'd realized his feelings for her. She wouldn't believe him if he were to tell her. For women like Sherri, things had to be proven and he had time to do just that.

The Holy Terror *way.* If he had been persistent before, then she hadn't seen anything yet.

Deciding not to argue with her about their future, he said, "Okay, I can see your point. Have a nice day, and I'm sure I'll see you sometime this week at the station."

He then leaned over and placed a kiss on her lips before heading toward his own car.

Chapter 8

"Hey, Key West, this is the Holy Terror and you're tuned in to WLCK, 101.5 on your radio dial. *Sports Talk* is about you, the sports-enthusiast, and today we're going to take your questions and facilitate your discussions on whether you think the Yankees have a snowball's chance in hell of winning the World Series this year. Personally, I don't think they do, so if you disagree call in and tell me why."

Sherri smiled as she parked her car in the spot usually reserved for her uncle. Like a number of people around town, she was enjoying Terrence on the air, although she wouldn't call herself a "sports-enthusiast." Point-blank, she enjoyed listening to the sound of his voice. It was husky, masculine, with a low rumble that could conjure erotic thoughts in any woman's head—and probably did, considering the show's high ratings. A number of callers were women, and you couldn't convince her that that many women in the Keys were interested in sports.

Depends on what you're playing, she thought, remembering their fantasy game of two nights ago. Not only had he played exceedingly well, but he had served up something so passionate that she felt her temperature rising just thinking about it.

Had it been two nights ago? No wonder her body was still in a state of sensual heat. She couldn't even go to bed at night without remembering what they had shared. The man had an intense sexual appetite, and the more he was fed the more he had wanted. And she had obliged, learning a number of things in the process. Like you could have multiple orgasms and that there was such a thing as an erogenous zone, because he had definitely tapped into hers that night.

So what was next? Nothing. She was determined more than ever to move on and tuck away those special memories of their night together. With him out of her system, she would be able to do just that. She understood the yearnings she still experienced at night at bedtime and often during the day. Any woman who had been made love to as thoroughly as she had would suffer periods of loss. She could handle it as long as it didn't get to the point where she was driven to act on it.

That wouldn't be done. Terrence had gotten what he had wanted from her, and she had basically gotten what she wanted from him. They were adults and would act accordingly.

She looked at the clock on her dashboard. The U.S. National Hurricane Service had announced that Tropical Storm Ana had formed over the Dominican Republic and was expected to head west toward Cuba over the weekend. If the storm strengthened it could become the first hurricane of the season. Currently, there was less than a thirty percent chance of that happening, but everyone was still keeping their eyes on Ana just the same. WLCK had an excellent news department, and she wanted to make sure that their station was where listeners would call in to get the most up-to-date and reliable weather reports. To make sure that was in place, she would hold a meeting later that day with Prentice Sherman, the station's meteorologist.

She had gotten a call from Uncle Warrick that morning reporting that the negotiations with Jeremy

Wilkins were going slowly. Wilkins, who knew just how much Warrick wanted the Memphis radio station, was trying to be difficult, although it would be in the man's best interest to sell. Uncle Warrick was determined to wait things out, soften the man up a little and make him another offer at the beginning of next week. Meanwhile, she'd keep everything at the station under control.

Getting out of her car, Sherri could immediately feel the change in the air and hoped that the tropical storm would not be coming their way.

Terrence glanced at the clock on the wall. He only had time for one more call, and he hoped it was a short one. After the show was over he intended to drop by Sherri's office to see how she was doing. He had deliberately kept his distance for two days, trying to be a nice guy and give her space before he moved in and started gobbling it up. Just thinking about how he intended to do it made him smile. Sherri Griffin wouldn't know what hit her until she was back in his bed again. But he didn't intend to stop there. He had plans for them, plans he would have to orchestrate without her knowing he was doing so. For the first time in his life, he wanted to do more with a woman than sleep with her.

The monitor in front of him started to blink, indicating he had another call. His last one for the day. He rolled his eyes. It was Monica Kendricks. She liked to call in and flirt with him over the air. In the past he hadn't minded as long as no rules were broken. But that was before Sherri.

He plugged into the call. "Thanks for holding, Monica. So tell me, who do you think will win the World Series?"

Her husky, feminine laughter grated on his nerves today. "I'm going to go with the Cowboys."

He couldn't help but chuckle. "Wrong sport. Cowboys are a football team."

"Oh. Is there any way to tell them apart other than the balls they play with?"

He frowned, thinking that was really a dumb question and covered the mike with his hand when Mark, who was manning the booth, let out a gigantic laugh.

He shot Mark a glare although he was fighting to keep from laughing himself. "Yes, there're also the rules of the game, which are totally different, and the uniforms the players wear. Typically there aren't any cheerleaders for baseball and—"

"Why not?"

"Excuse me?"

"Why aren't there cheerleaders for baseball?"

This time Terrence did chuckle. "Now that's a question for another day. Callers, if any of you know the answer to Monica's question, call in on Friday. You will be listening, won't you, Monica?"

"I always listen to you, Holy Terror. And I'm thinking about coming to your club tonight."

He rolled his eyes again. "You do that. We could use the business. Thanks for calling in." Before she could say anything else, he quickly disconnected the line.

"That's it for today. Join me again on Friday so we can see how many of you will be able to answer Monica's question—why don't baseball teams have cheerleaders?" Terrence said to the listening audience as he closed out the show. "Until then, peace and stay safe."

He then switched off the control, turned off his mike and was about to remove his headset when Mark's voice transmitted through one of the speakers. "That woman definitely has the hots for you, Holy Terror. I wonder what she looks like."

He laughed. "Why don't you drop by the club tonight and see?"

"Um, you think she'll show up?"

A lazy grin spread over Terrence's face. "Yes, she'll show up."

"I hate to mess up any plans you might have for her," Mark said. Terrence didn't have to look in the man's direction to know he probably had a smirk on his face. Twenty-five years old and divorced, the young man was working two jobs while trying to go to school and paying child support for one child. Mark had hit the dating scene again running and hadn't slowed down since.

"You won't be messing up any of my plans because I'm not interested. But she might be too old for you," he said to Mark.

"That's okay with me. I've decided to date older women for a while. I heard they're less trouble and lower maintenance."

Terrence shook his head and decided not to intervene. He'd discovered long ago that experience was the best teacher. "Good luck."

He removed his headset and leaned back in his chair. He had to admit that he enjoyed doing the show. It only took a few hours of his time twice a week and it got him out of the club so he wouldn't get in CC's way. But now, with Sherri on his agenda, that meant he had less time to kill. And whether she knew it or not, she was on his agenda. As high up there as any woman could get and ever would get.

He glanced at his watch. He had dropped by her

office earlier, and she had posted a note on her door that she had left the station to go to an off-site meeting. He wondered if she had returned and decided there was only one way to find out.

Sherri turned off the radio in her office, thinking that the woman who had called in had openly flirted with Terrence and he had flirted back. Okay, he hadn't flirted back, exactly, but when Monica What's-her-name said that she would be showing up at Terrence's club tonight, he had indicated she should do that because he could use the business…a business that didn't have an advertising spot on his show.

She got up from her desk, refusing to admit she was being a little bit unreasonable. Or that she was just a teeny bit angry at the woman. And at Terrence.

And she outright, positively refused to consider that she was jealous.

She began pacing while thinking that she was too much of a professional to do something like that. Her anger had nothing to do with Terrence; what he did on his own time was his business. She just didn't like the fact that he'd given a plug for his club on the air.

"May I come in?"

At the sound of the deep, husky male voice, she whirled around to find the object of her anger standing there in the open doorway. And of all the nerve, he was smiling. Why hadn't she closed her door? If she had, then he could have assumed she'd been busy and would not have disturbed her. And today he was disturbing her. This was the first time she had been in his presence since the night they had rolled around between the sheets and the morning when they had made love in her shower. Just thinking about both suddenly made her feel so hot she wanted to remove her jacket, but she refrained from doing so.

"It seems you're already in," she said after he closed the door and walked across the threshold.

Her smart response only widened his smile, showing that dangerously sexy dimple. It was the same dimple that, in the heat of the moment, she had licked several times.

She inhaled deeply. Now was not the time to think about what the two of them had done two nights ago, about the sensations his lovemaking had evoked, about the numerous orgasms she'd had. And for the first time ever.

"How are you today, Sherri?"

His question interrupted her thoughts, which was a good thing. "I'm doing fine, and you?"

"I'm doing fine, as well, but if you want you can ask me how I can be better."

She tried ignoring the stirring in the pit of her stomach when listening to the deep, husky tone of his voice. "And why would I want to do that?"

"Um, I can think of several reasons."

She frowned at him. He was hinting about the time they had spent together, and she wished he wouldn't go there. Although she didn't regret anything they had done, it was over and there wouldn't be any repeats. They had wanted one night and they had gotten it. However, the lazy grin that appeared on his face reminded her that they had gotten more than one night if you took into consideration the morning after in the shower, which had resulted in them tumbling back in bed between the sheets again afterward.

"Well, I can't think of any reasons," she finally said and decided to quickly change the subject. "I listened to your talk show today."

She figured that there must have been something in her voice that put him on alert. He braced his jean-clad legs apart in that stance she always found sexy and crossed his arms over his chest. "And?" he asked, the single word a husky rumble from his throat.

She lifted her chin. "And I think you got out of line with Monica What's-her-name."

"Kendricks. It's Monica Kendricks, and she's a frequent caller to the show. And how did I get out of line with her?"

She inhaled deeply, knowing in all actuality she shouldn't go there, especially after Warrick had explained on her first day that Terrence's performance and anything related to it was his concern and not hers. But Warrick was out of town and had left her in charge. Surely she had the authority to provide Terrance with whatever feedback she felt was warranted.

"She flirted with you," she heard herself saying.

If the smile he sent her way was any indication, he seemed amused by that observation. "Yes, she flirted with me," he agreed. "She's not the first caller who has and probably won't be the last." He leaned back against a file cabinet. "So what's your point?"

Now she was the one who crossed her arms over her chest. "My point is that you flirted back."

Another amused smile touched his lips. "You think so?"

"Yes, and that was a very unprofessional thing to do."

Terrence studied Sherri's face, and when he saw she was dead serious, he had to refrain from chuckling. "And what do you think was so unprofessional about it?" he asked, needing to know just where she was coming from.

"You encouraged her."

"I encouraged her?"

"Yes."

This, he thought, was getting good. "And just how was she encouraged?" He could feel the vibes coming from her, and she wasn't a happy camper.

"When she said she was coming to your club tonight, you told her to do that and that the club could use the business. Not only was such a statement unprofessional, but since you haven't purchased any advertisement time for your club, it was unethical."

Terrence looked down at his shoes. He could deal with a lot, but for someone to take him to task for something as silly as this was a waste of his time. He had come into her office to kiss her, not to tangle with her, although he would just love tackling her to the floor about now and working that skirt up her waist, getting rid of her panties and—

"Just so you know, I'm going to mention the incident to Warrick when he returns, since you report directly to him. But in the meantime, until he gets back I'd appreciate it if you'd conduct yourself appropriately," she interrupted his thoughts by adding.

He shook his head, deciding she really did need to use her lips and tongue for something other than talking.

"Conduct myself appropriately?" he asked, as if savoring each word, every single syllable.

"That would be appreciated."

With an inward sigh, he straightened his tall frame and crossed the floor to cover the short distance separating them. "And you're upset because a woman came on to me?"

"That's not it at all. Women can do what they want to you or with you. That's not my concern, although I'm curious as to how many of our listeners will show up tonight at your club to see for themselves just how you conduct yourself with her. She's been calling in for practically every show. Everyone knows the only interest she has in sports is you."

He reached out and pushed a few strands of hair out of her face. "And this bothers you." It was more a statement than a question, and he knew she would take it as such.

Sherri rolled her eyes. "Don't try making this personal, Terrence."

He smiled. "I don't have to make it personal since you're doing a very good job of it for me. Would it make you feel better if I told you that I don't plan on going to the club tonight?"

"It doesn't matter to me what you do."

A devilish gleam appeared in his eyes. "In that case, I'll see you later tonight."

Sherri blinked, certain she had missed something along the way. "Excuse me?"

"No need, you didn't do anything."

She took a step, got in his face. "And what makes you think you can just come over to my place?"

Terrence couldn't stop smiling. She looked cute when she was angry. "Because you said you don't care what I do," he reminded her. "On that note, I might as well take it a little further, since it seems you're mad at me anyway."

Before a frown could set in her face, Terrence lowered his head and took her mouth, laying claim to whatever biting words she was about to say, effectively wiping them from her lips. Once his tongue slid into her mouth, her response was instantaneous. And when his tongue began moving around her mouth in long, fluid strokes, he heard her moan.

The sound made fire gush through his bloodstream, and he reached out and placed his arms around her waist to draw her closer. He then shifted his hand to cup her backside, liking the feel of that part of her in his hand even through her clothes. His tongue had been playing a cat-and-mouse game with hers, and when it was finally within her grasp, she surprised him and sucked on it in a way that nearly brought him to his knees. But he refused to buckle. He needed to stand upright to torment her mouth the way she was tormenting his.

The palm of his hand glided sensuously back and forth over her cute bottom, kneading it tenderly, while at the same time the hardness of his erection pressed against her stomach. An ache throbbed to life inside him, and it wouldn't take much to push him over the edge and have him take her right there on her desk.

There was no telling how long they would have continued to kiss if there hadn't been a loud knock on the door. Her breath caught the moment Terrence released her mouth. He watched as she breathed in deeply, fighting the urge to kiss her again.

A knock sounded again, and she quickly went to the door, glancing over her shoulder before making a move to open it. Since a hard-on was something he knew couldn't go away quickly, he decided to sit down on the love seat. "Go ahead and open the door, Sherri," he said quietly. "I'm as put together as I can get under the circumstances."

Trying to recoup all her senses, Sherri took a deep breath before opening the door to find Prentice Sherman standing there. It was then that she remembered their meeting. She cleared her throat. "Prentice, sorry about this, but my meeting with Terrence has run over for just a bit. I'll buzz you when we're finished."

Prentice smiled. "Sure thing, Sherri. No problem. I'll be in the break room," he said before turning to leave.

As soon as the door was closed, Sherri whirled around and stared at Terrence with eyes as sharp as daggers. "How dare you."

An innocent look appeared on his face. "How dare I what? Kiss you? In that case, how dare you kiss me back?"

Inhaling a calming breath, or at least trying to do so, she ran her fingers through the mass of hair on her head. There was no way Prentice wasn't suspicious about what they had been doing. First, it had taken two knocks before she had opened the door, and then there was no doubt in her mind that she probably looked like a woman who'd been pretty well kissed.

"This is all a game to you, isn't it, Terrence?"

"Why would you think that?" he asked, getting to his feet.

"Because it was my understanding that after our one night together there would be no more hitting on me. No more trying to get me in your bed. No more of anything. We *did* it."

Terrence couldn't stop the smile that touched his lips when he crossed the room to stand in front of her. "Yes, we did do it, and it was done in a way that still leaves me breathless whenever I think about it. And for that reason, I need to spend more time with you. I need to do it again."

"No. Once was enough."

He shook his head. "No, once wasn't enough for me, and from your response to our kiss, not for you, either."

She lifted her chin. "You're imagining things."

Amusement darted across his lips. "Trust me, whenever I'm inside your mouth or inside your body, I'm dealing strictly with reality."

He checked his watch. "It's getting late, so I'll leave you to meet with Prentice. I'll call you later to see if—"

"Don't."

He met her gaze, and she met his. "Why are you afraid of me?" he asked softly.

"Leery is a better word, and like I said earlier, I refuse to participate in whatever game you're playing."

He thought about the game they'd willingly

played together two nights ago. Their naked bodies tumbling between soft cotton sheets… His mouth tasting the sweetness of her unlimited times with no threat of facing a time-out… Her body while her inner muscles clenched him inside of her, releasing him and then clenching him some more, milking him for everything he had… He no longer had to wonder how it would be to make love to her, because now he knew. That knowledge stirred his insides whenever he thought about it. It was the force behind the hunger, so intense and deep, it racked his senses. It was part of what was channeling his love, something he could admit to freely.

"Do we understand each other, Terrence?"

Her question regained his attention, and he felt it was important that she be the one to understand. He wouldn't tell her that he had fallen in love with her until he had time to work on her heart. Whatever glass case she had surrounding it would be broken into tiny pieces. "Once wasn't enough, Sherri. I want you again. And again. But I'm willing to give you time to adjust to the idea. I'll see you on Friday."

And without giving her a chance to respond, he headed for the door.

Chapter 9

"Have you been keeping up with the weather report?"

Sherri glanced across the restaurant table at Kim and wiped her mouth before she spoke. "I can't help but keep up with it. We have a meteorologist at the station, and I met with him today. At four o'clock the most recent update from the National Weather Service indicated there was a possibility that Ana could strengthen significantly when she emerges from Cuba's north coast. If that happens, then she has a chance of becoming a hurricane and could pass near here."

"That's scary."

Sherri nodded. Neither she nor Kim had ever lived in a place that was this close to a hurricane's breeding ground.

"Well, there's nothing we can do. It's all in the hands of Mother Nature, but I'm hoping it bypasses here," Kim said.

Sherri couldn't help but agree. Deciding to change the subject, she asked Kim about the doctor she was dating. "He's okay," Kim said, shrugging her shoulders. "He's been divorced twice and that might not be a good sign, but I'm willing to go out with him a few more times. He likes to have fun, and that's good, although I think he's also dating another doctor."

Sherri lifted her brow. "And how do you feel about that?"

Kim shrugged. "Doesn't bother me, since we're not exclusive. What about you and the Holy Terror?"

Sherri glanced over at Kim. "What about us?" Kim knew he had spent the night, so Sherri knew that wasn't what she was inquiring about.

"So you admit there's an 'us'?"

Sherri shook her head. "No, it was a slip of the tongue, nothing more, although he evidently thinks there's an us. We clearly went into that night knowing it was a one-night stand, but now he wants a repeat."

Kim's eyes widened. "Really? Everything I've read said he doesn't do repeats."

"Then what about that socialite he'd become involved with?" If anyone knew the details, Kim would. Her best friend lived and breathed the Internet when she wasn't working. Sherri sometimes thought it was a wonder she'd never taken a job with the FBI, since Kim had such a keen investigative nature.

"Oh, he only dated her those few times as a favor to her father, this real-estate tycoon on the island. Evidently she put more stock into the affair—if you really want to call it that—than Holy Terror did. After a few dates, when she began to get clingy, he cut her loose, but not before she'd told everyone they were engaged and he was having her ring sized. I'm told her lie pissed him off and he embarrassed her by retracting her claim. End of story."

Sherri took a sip of her drink and said nothing.

Kim asked after a moment, "So what do you plan to do? You know how persistent he is."

Sherri nodded. Yes, she knew. "I'll keep telling him no. Eventually he'll get the message."

"Don't be surprised if he doesn't. I think you made quite an impression on him."

Sherri rolled her eyes. "Whatever."

She really didn't care what sort of impression she might have made on Terrence. The bottom line was that a one-night stand was a one-night stand, and she had no intention of modifying their agreement.

When the live band began playing, she decided to try and put any thoughts of Terrence from her mind, but she couldn't help wondering what he was doing now. Had he not gone to the club tonight to meet the infamous Monica Kendricks like he'd said or had he gone?

She wanted to kick herself for caring whether he went. And for caring about the man himself. Though she had admitted to having feelings for him, it was something he would never know. The man was too arrogant already.

Terrence placed the book he'd been reading on the nightstand and then shifted positions in bed. He had just finished talking to Stephen, who told him the auhorities were gearing up for a mass evacuation because of Ana if one was officially called.

The last time he had talked to Lucas was a few days ago. His friend was waiting for Emma to fly in, hoping she would make it before the flights got canceled. Terrence hadn't wanted to tell Lucas not to hold his breath waiting for the woman since she had promised to fly in numerous other times and hadn't made an appearance yet.

Terrence smiled, thinking how his father, Olivia and Duan had called to make sure everything was okay. They had heard about the tropical storm on the radio and had been concerned.

He had assured them that he was fine and that chances were the storm would shift and move in another direction. At least he was hoping that would be the case. The Dominican Republic was presently taking a beating, but all they were getting in the Keys was a lot of strong wind. Still, he knew that would be changing if the dark clouds were any indication.

Speaking of dark, he couldn't help but remember the dark frown that had been on Sherri's face when he had walked out of her office earlier. To say he had riled her anger was an understatement.

He shifted in bed again and decided the next time they made love would be over here at his place, in this very bed. No other woman had set foot in his bedroom, but he intended for her to be the first as well as the last. He wondered what she would think about that. In her current mood, she wouldn't think much about it. She'd denounce the very idea that such a thing might ever happen. But whatever it took, he would make sure it happened.

He would love to have her in bed beneath him when she wouldn't be thinking at all, just enjoying the moment. He intended to have that and more. Sherri Griffin might be stubborn, but when it came to implementing plays and rushing them to the goal line, she would discover no one was better than him.

He glanced over at the phone. He was tempted to call her, but he wouldn't. He would give her a couple of days to get adjusted to the idea of what was going on between them. He had broken down her defenses once and intended to do so again.

He wouldn't be satisfied until he not only had Sherri in his bed, but had her as a permanent fixture in his life. He intended to make her his.

Listeners, this is Prentice Sherman, meteorologist at WLCK, and this is another update from the U.S. National Hurricane Center in Miami. All eyes are on Tropical Storm Ana. She has been responsible for at least four deaths in the Dominican Republic. It seems things aren't favorable for us as forecasters have predicted that once Ana passes over Cuba, she will make landfall here in the Keys in two to three days, at which time it is expected she will reach hurricane status. Official evacuation plans are now under way. Residents and tourists are urged to heed evacuation directions.

Sherri stood in her office and looked out the window. The wind had picked up, and the palm trees were swaying back and forth. Coming in to work, she had encountered more traffic on the roadway than ever. Everyone was taking heed of the weather warning. Ana was still a tropical storm but was expected to reach hurricane status by landfall in a couple of days. Since most of South Florida was in Ana's path, the governor had already declared a state of emergency. This morning, tourists had been asked to leave the Keys, and those living in low-lying areas and mobile homes would be evacuating in a timely manner.

She had spoken with Uncle Warrick earlier today and he indicated he would be staying put in Memphis and would depend on her to keep things running in his absence. A lot had been placed on her shoulders, but she was ready to handle things.

The station had received a lot of calls from frantic listeners wanting to know what to do and where to go. According to Prentice, who had lived in the Keys all his life and was used to hurricane evacuations, the most important thing the station could do was to keep providing updates and to maintain business as usual. If they panicked, then the listeners would panic. For that reason, programming would remain the same, other than breaks for periodic updates on the storm. Terrence was due to hit the air in a few minutes.

Terrence.

She tried not to let thoughts of him overtake her mind. Today was the first day she had seen him since that time he had spent in her office. The day he had kissed her with a passion that made her toes curl. Earlier, she had held a meeting with everyone to advise them of her decision not to make any changes in programming.

Like everyone else, he hadn't said much, but she did notice the way he had looked at her and the smile he had given her. It was as if he'd known the importance of what needed to be done under her authority and was sending her his silent support. At least that's what she assumed his smile had meant, but with Terrence one never really knew.

She turned from the window when she heard the knock on her office door. "Come in."

Prentice stuck his head in. "Hey, I just wanted to let you know of our most recent update. Ana is now officially a Category One hurricane."

Sherri nodded. "And her path hasn't shifted?" she asked, hoping that it had.

He shook his head. "No, although she seems to be a slow-moving gal. She was expected to leave Cuba hours ago, but she has decided to linger. That's good for us but bad for Cuba."

He looked at his watch. "Next radio update isn't for another thirty minutes, during *Sports Talk*."

"Okay, and thanks. I know you've been putting in a lot of hours during the past couple of days, and it is appreciated."

He smiled and said "Thanks" before closing the door behind him.

She did appreciate him. He was one of the first people Warrick had introduced her to. Prentice and his wife, Lucinda, were expecting their first child next month.

Satisfied everything was running smoothly, she went back to her desk and turned on the console to listen to *Sports Talk*.

"This is the Holy Terror and you've tuned in to another edition of *Sports Talk* at WLCK. Just in case you haven't heard, Ana is now a Category One hurricane and forecasters have predicted the lady is headed our way. During today's show we will give you periodic updates because the last thing we want you to do is get caught unawares."

He leaned back in his chair and said, "Today's show will pick up where we left off when one of our listeners asked the question why there aren't any cheerleaders for baseball. Phone in with your comments. We're going to take our first call after the station identifies itself."

Terrence flipped the switch to break for a commercial and took that time to sip his coffee. He glanced around. At first when Warrick had talked him into taking the job, the small soundproof studio where the DJs broadcasted their shows and from where *Sports Talk* would be aired had bothered him. He was a man used to space. But over the past year he'd gotten used to it and actually looked forward to being inside the booth. It was peaceful, relaxing, and other than Mark, who was holed up in the glass-enclosed booth next to him, he was virtually alone.

Alone with his thoughts.

When he had seen Sherri earlier today, his reaction to her had been instantaneous. Immediately, there had been a stirring in his gut, and his heart had pounded hard and heavy in his chest. She had called a meeting, and in that professional way of hers, she had brought everyone up to date on Ana.

She had surprised everyone by actually dressing down today with her jeans and polo shirt. Still, she had managed to look professional anyway. This was the first time he'd seen her in jeans, and she looked good in them, especially the way the denim emphasized her curvy backside. He was going to have to encourage her to dress down more often.

He sighed as he checked the commercial reel to find he had less than a minute left. He glanced over to see Mark looking through some girly magazine. According to Mark, Monica had shown up that night at Club Hurricane, and she was a looker. A woman in her thirties, she had seemed disappointed that Terrence hadn't been there to greet her. Terrence had chuckled at that, thinking she would get over it.

"Five seconds to airtime, Holy Terror."

Mark's voice interrupted his thoughts, and he turned his attention back to the business at hand.

"Welcome back. This is the Holy Terror, and you're listening to *Sports Talk* on WLCK. Today's topic is why there aren't cheerleaders for baseball." He pressed the button for line one. "Okay, Stan, what's your opinion?" Stan was a regular, and Terrence hadn't been surprised he'd called.

"Hey, Holy Terror, I think there aren't any cheerleaders for baseball because of the danger," Stan said.

Terrence raised a brow. "Danger?"

"Yes. A ball off a bat is more likely to hit a cheerleader and cause serious damage than a basketball, soccer ball or football."

Terrence nodded. "Um, you have a point there, Stan. Thanks for calling to provide your input."

He then clicked on line two. "Okay, next caller, what do you think?"

"I think it's a good question, and a good idea. It will get the fans into the game and give them something a lot prettier to look at than a player chewing tobacco and then spitting on the ground. How disgusting."

Terrence couldn't help but chuckle at that. "Well, every sport has its own idiosyncrasies. Thanks for calling in with your comment."

He disconnected the call, and instead of taking another, he said, "Now it's time for a weather update with Prentice Sherman." He pushed a button to bring Prentice, who was in another sound room, on the air. He then turned off the mike.

He leaned back in his chair while keeping an eye

on the computer monitor that would tell him when to reconnect. He wondered what Sherri was doing. He knew that with Warrick away she had her hands full. Any thoughts about getting her to let him into her space would have to be placed on the back burner for a while. Hurricane Ana was the main thing on everyone's mind right now.

Chapter 10

Sherri studied the flashing computer screen on her desk while tightening her grip on the phone in her hand. "I understand, Prentice. Your first priority is to Lucinda and to get her to the hospital. Be careful and call me when you find out something."

She hung up the phone and took deep breaths. Prentice had called to say Lucinda had started spotting and the doctor had suggested he take her to the hospital since the baby wasn't due for another month. That meant WLCK wouldn't have a weatherman.

She slumped down in her chair. On top of everything else, two other employees, including Mark, had phoned to say they couldn't come. As far as she knew, the only person at the station, other than herself, was Soul Man, the DJ who was currently spinning the *Old School Hour*. He had been doing a good job of providing weather updates, but he'd been there for twelve hours already, and she couldn't ask him to stay any longer. Besides, her employees needed to go home and take care of personal business. They had lives outside the radio station. That meant she would be doing the solo act for a while. She had no other choice since she refused to go on total autopilot. She'd let music run on autopilot, but she'd stay to give updates on the weather.

She sighed again when she heard the phone ring, wondering if things were about to get worse. "Hello."

"Sherri, it's Kim. I just took a quick break to make sure you're okay."

"I'm as well as can be expected." She told Kim about the call-ins.

"Maybe you ought to follow their lead and go home," Kim said seriously.

Sherri shook her head. "I can't do that. As long as the station stays on the air, I will be here. I packed an overnight bag before I left this morning and brought in extra clothes, so I intend to stay put.

Besides, with all the generators in place I'll probably do better here."

"What about your personal belongings?"

"Since I'm on the second floor my apartment should be fine. It's a new complex and, according to my landlord, built to withstand a lot more wind than we're expecting."

She looked at the clock on her wall. "Look, Kim, I need to go. Soul Man is getting off at four today, and I need to take over. I don't want him to think I'll keep him here unnecessarily."

"Okay, you take care."

"You do the same, Kim."

Sherri stood. For the second straight day she had worn jeans in to work, a decision she hadn't been pleased with at the time. But the owner of her local dry cleaner—where most of her business suits were still hanging—had feared Ana's predicted fury and closed the shop and caught the first plane leaving the Keys. Sherri had been surprised since most of the other business owners in the area were adamant about waiting it out and didn't plan to close shop until it became absolutely necessary.

She had searched her closet and had been forced to do some quick shopping at the mall down the street after discovering she didn't own a pair of jeans.

Now she had come to the conclusion they weren't so bad and were rather comfortable. Hard habits just weren't easy to break.

She crossed the room, stepped out into the corridor and immediately collided with the hard bulk of someone's body. She knew in an instant, the moment a hand went to her waist to steady her, whose body it was. Terrence.

"You okay?"

The concern she heard in the deep, husky voice almost made her weep, in light of the load she had on her shoulders. Instead, she straightened those shoulders and met his eyes, trying to ignore just how good he looked…as usual.

"Yes, I'm okay. What are you doing here? Didn't you get the message not to come in?" Programming had changed due to the storm and *Sports Talk* was canceled today.

He leaned against the wall. "Yes, I got the message."

She frowned. "Then why are you here?"

He smiled. "I'm here, Sherri, because you're here. I got a call from Prentice and he told me about Lucinda. I knew that would leave you in a tough spot since, according to Prentice, you're not putting the station on total autopilot. So I came in to help."

"In this weather? You came in here?" she asked incredulously.

"Yes."

That didn't make any sense, which pushed her to ask, "What about your club? It's on the ocean. Don't you have to board it up or something? You have an entire back wall that's nothing but glass."

"There was no need," he said easily. "I had hurricane shutters installed a few years ago. Besides, I have people in place to take care of whatever needs to be done."

He looked her up and down and then said, "I like your outfit, by the way. I meant to tell you the other day how good you look in jeans."

She swallowed against the thickness in her throat as well as the fluttering in her stomach. "Thanks."

"So what can I do to help? I've pitched in for Prentice before, so I'm available if you need me to do weather updates."

She sighed deeply. Although she didn't want to admit it, considering her lack of manpower, he was a godsend. "You can do that, but that means you'll also have to be the DJ since Hercules called to say he can't come in and Soul Man has been here for twelve hours already, so there's no way I can ask him to stay any longer."

He nodded. "Where's Mark?"

She shook her head. "Not coming in, either."

"So it was just going to be you here alone handling things?"

At her nod he let out a curse. "Why didn't you just place the station on autopilot and let music play for the next twenty-four to seventy-two hours or longer? With all the modern technology, this station can be programmed to basically run itself, so what are you trying to prove by placing yourself in danger?" he asked in an angry tone.

She glared up at him. "I'm not trying to prove anything. There are people out there, still left in their homes, displaced in hotels, who are tuned in to us and are depending on hearing what we have to tell them about the weather. They need periodic updates that can only come from a live body."

When she saw from his expression that her words hadn't gotten through to him because he knew she was still holding something back, she glanced down at the floor for a moment before looking back up to meet his gaze. "Okay, maybe I do feel I have something to prove, Terrence. I'm running things in Warrick's absence, and I need to come through on this. I have to prove to him and to myself that I can do it."

Why she had shared that with him she wasn't sure. Maybe the stress was getting to her. But she was determined to prevail.

He didn't say anything for a minute. He just stood there and stared at her. Then he smiled and squeezed her shoulder lightly before placing his arm around her. "Okay, then, let's go relieve Soul Man."

Soul Man was out of there in a flash once they took over. Because Terrence was familiar with the setup, he took over as DJ and Sherri went to work to make sure they were connected to the Hurricane Center for periodic feedback. Once in the glass-enclosed booth, she also checked the equipment to handle incoming calls, making sure it was working properly and at full capacity.

Because they'd moved to work fast, she hadn't given herself time to ponder the fact that she and Terrence were the only two at the station, confined against the approaching storm. So far, there were only high winds and debris flying around, but from the look of the dark clouds, rain was coming. It was imperative that everyone understood the severity of the hurricane and took precautions. She hoped Terrence used his time and influence on the air to stress that to everyone.

He glanced over at her and smiled before putting on his headset. The autopilot was in place to play continuous music with Terrence breaking in every so often to give updates on the weather.

She just wished she wasn't getting that funny feeling in her stomach every time he smiled at her and showed that dimple. The last thing she needed to remember was the night and morning they had made love. She hadn't known just how thorough his mouth had been until she had gotten undressed later that day and found passion marks practically everywhere, especially in the area between her thighs.

Terrence's voice on the airwaves interrupted her thoughts.

"Hey, folks, this is Holy Terror sitting in for the Mighty Hercules. I'll be the voice of calm on your radio and will keep you updated on that voracious hurricane out there, and yes, Ana is acting like a scorned woman, kicking everything in her path, and is presently kicking Cuba's you-know-what."

Sherri placed her hand over her face and cringed. Although he hadn't used profanity, no one had to imagine just what he meant. She glanced over at him, caught his eye and shook her head, letting him know he needed to tone it down. He merely chuckled and continued talking to the audience.

"I'm here with the station's beautiful program director, Sherri Griffin, and she will be assisting me in making sure you get the hurricane facts on a periodic basis. I know many of you thought that you could stay put, but now that's not an option. So get your butts in gear and evacuate. For those who refuse to leave, you need to take every precaution."

Sherri's eyes widened, not believing that Terrence had said "get your butts in gear."

She placed her hand on her forehead. She felt a headache coming on.

Terrence glanced over at Sherri in the glass booth. He didn't intend for her to stay there for long, since there was no need for her to distance herself from him with the station basically operating on its own. For now he would give her the space she evidently wanted, but with just the two of them at the station, he was overflowing with ideas about how they could spend their free time. He no longer had to wonder how it would be to make love to her because he knew and had a burning desire to do so again. His body was getting hard just thinking about it.

Deciding for the time being to switch his thoughts elsewhere, he checked his watch and wondered how Stephen was doing. He had talked to him earlier. An article had appeared in the papers proclaiming Stephen a hero after rescuing some careless tourists from their car that had plunged down a ravine. He'd gotten hurt and sustained a few cuts and bruises, but after a night spent in the hospital, he seemed to be doing fine. And Terrence also needed to give Lucas a call to see if Emma had made it in, although Terrence had a feeling she hadn't, as usual. He and Stephen had had several talks with Lucas regarding why his fiancée never showed up when she was supposed to. As far as he was concerned, Lucas was putting more into this long-distance relationship than his fiancée.

Music was continuously playing, a mixture of everything: old school, hip-hop, rap and R & B. Currently Tamia was blowing out a number entitled "So Into You." He smiled, deciding he was going to make that his theme song in pursuit of Sherri and wondered if she was listening to the lyrics. Probably not, since she was messing around with the transmitter board, not even paying him any attention.

It was time she became his captive audience.

"Sherri, could you come here for a minute, please?"

Sherri inhaled deeply upon hearing the deep, husky voice coming through her headset. She refused to shift her gaze away from the computer monitor. She had known the moment Terrence's eyes had lit on her. She had felt it in the way her body had responded and hadn't wanted to give in to temptation and look back. But now she couldn't help herself and tilted her head to look in his direction.

The moment their eyes connected, she'd known it was a mistake.

Need. An overwhelming craving began stirring in her middle and was working its way down her body. Once it reached the area between her legs, she had to tighten her thighs together to find relief. Not that she got any. Terrence had the ability to make her burn…for nobody other than for him.

She slowly released her breath when his voice came in again through her headset. His eyes still locked with hers. "Come here, Sherri."

She swallowed and somehow found her voice. "Why?"

"I need you to do me a favor."

She broke eye contact with him to look back at the computer monitor, trying to resist the pull the sound of his deep, sexy voice had on her. What kind of favor did he need her to do? It had to be about business and not pleasure, right? She didn't want to ask for fear of giving him any ideas.

She figured if she didn't go see what he wanted, he would only ask again, so removing her headset and pushing back her chair, she stood and walked out of the safe haven of the glass booth. His eyes were on her every step she took. She tried looking away but couldn't.

When she came within a few feet of where he was sitting, she couldn't help noticing how his gaze roamed her up and down before zeroing back on her eyes with targetlike precision. And like a bull's-eye getting pierced by an arrow, she felt the direct hit in every part of her body, especially between her thighs.

"What kind of favor?" she asked, watching him continue to study her.

"Stay in here. Keep me company," he said, shifting his gaze to her mouth and pulling out the chair beside his. At that moment she couldn't help but remember the last kiss they had shared, the heat it had generated, the moans she had made.

"I don't think that's a good idea," she said, struggling to put more punch behind her words. "Besides, I have work to do." She knew the latter sounded like the lie it was.

"I think it's a good idea," he interrupted her thoughts by saying. "And as far as you having work to do, how about coming up with another excuse?"

Her lips firmed into a line. "I don't have to make excuses for not wanting to spend time with you, Terrence."

He nodded. "No, you don't. But I would think, considering everything, that you could spare a few moments of your time. You and I are the only two people here."

Sherri wished he hadn't reminded her. She looked around and noticed just how quiet things were. Except for the sound of Ashford and Simpson, all was peaceful. She looked at the monitor as she sat down. "It's time for a weather update, and you have a call coming in."

He followed her gaze and looked at the monitor. "All right." He put on his headset and turned on his mike.

"Hey, folks, this is the Holy Terror with a weather update. Those of you hoping Ana would turn west and spare us a devastating blow may not get your wish. Don't defy the evacuation order that's been put in effect any longer. According to the authorities, anyone refusing to leave—" he looked directly at Sherri "—is on their own."

He looked back at the monitor. "Now for an evacuation tip. Don't forget to get those important papers and special photographs in order and secure them in plastic. Hey, you guys, I wouldn't leave behind those divorce papers if I were you, and please don't forget those hidden pics of old girlfriends. Oh, yeah, you might want to go ahead and destroy that picture of your mother-in-law that you've been using for target practice."

Out of the corner of his eye he saw Sherri get out of her chair and come into his line of vision, furiously waving her hands. "Folks, we're going to have a commercial break and then I'll be back to take some calls. I see the board has lit up," he said into the mike. "Hold on. I definitely want to hear what you have to say."

As soon as he turned off the mike and removed his headset, she lit into him. "You can't say stuff like that!"

He lifted a brow. "And why can't I?"

"Because this is a serious matter," she snapped.

He checked the monitor to see how many minutes he had before pushing his chair back and standing. A hint of a smile touched his lips although he was trying to keep his temper in check. His woman was determined to drive him to drink.

His woman.

He liked the sound of that. He came to a stop in front of her and instead of stepping back she tilted her head back and glared up at him. "I think," he said slowly, "that I know when and how to take a hurricane seriously. I've been through a lot more of them than you have. And furthermore, those people out there are stressed, some are nervous, a lot of them are afraid. They need the humor. They appreciate it. So loosen up. You're wound up too tight."

"If I lose my job you will—"

"Jeez, you won't lose your job. Come here, you need me to help you relax." And before she could protest, he pulled her into his arms and captured the gasp that flowed from her mouth.

The moment their lips touched, she moaned. But so did he. It was like before. Like each and every time they kissed. She pulled something out of him. Something tangible. Deep. Passionate. He wondered at what point she would figure out that her mouth, lips and tongue belonged to him. So did every other part of her. Just like every part of him belonged to her.

He pulled his mouth away because he knew his time was up and he needed to go back to the monitor and take a few calls. "I want more," he murmured against her moist lips.

"You won't be getting it," she countered with a frown.

He lifted his head and smiled. The challenge was on.

* * *

Returning to the seat she had vacated earlier, Sherri watched how, with a smooth transition, Terrence went back on the air.

"Thanks for returning, folks. This is the Holy Terror filling in for the Mighty Hercules at WLCK, and I'm ready to take a call. Caller, what's on your mind?"

"Holy Terror, this is Fred. I agree with what you said about those pictures. I still have every flick I've taken of my old girlfriends."

Terrence chuckled. "Thanks for telling us, Fred. Have you evacuated yet?"

"Me and the old lady, we're moving to higher ground now."

"That's good to hear," Terrence said. "Stay safe."

He then went to the next call. "This is Holy Terror, what's on your mind?"

"Hey, Holy Terror, this is Agnes. Something else people need to grab before they evacuate is deeds to their property. Mine got washed away with the last hurricane, and I had the hardest time with my ex. He tried claiming my house was his."

"I hope you got things straightened out," Terrence said and took a sip out of his water bottle.

"I did. He's dead now."

Terrence choked when the water nearly went

down the wrong way. He cleared his throat. "He's dead?"

"But I didn't kill him. He died in bed with his young girlfriend."

Too much information. "Uh, sorry about that. Thanks for calling."

He disconnected the call. "Okay, folks, here's more music for your pleasure. The next weather update will be in about twenty minutes, along with another evacuation tip."

Sherri watched as he turned off the mike, removed his headset and glanced over at her before standing up and moving toward her.

Terrence's cell phone rang before be could pull Sherri into his arms. Muttering a curse, he pulled the phone out of his pocket, checking caller ID. "What's up, Stephen?"

"Just calling to let you know I think you're doing a great job at the station. I like your first tip."

Terrence smiled as his eyes remained on Sherri. "I thought you would. What's it like out there?"

Instead of getting a response, Terrence heard the screeching of brakes and then the sound of Stephen saying a few choice words before he came back on the phone. "You still there?" he asked Terrence.

"Yeah, I'm still here. What happened? Do you need me to send help your way?" Terrence asked, concerned. "I was just about to call in to police dispatch."

"No, I'm fine," Stephen said. After pausing a few minutes, he tacked on in a frustrated voice, "Do me a favor and reiterate that part about staying off the roads. Apparently your audience didn't hear it the first few times you mentioned it."

"What happened?"

"It's what didn't happen. A head-on collision."

"Come again?"

"I just had a near miss with some crazy lady speeding to get to an appointment in town," Stephen said angrily.

"But everything in town is closed," Terrence said.

"Yeah, I tried to tell her that," Stephen said, and Terrence could just see him shaking his head in disgust. "Listen, thanks for spreading the word about staying off the streets. Keep repeating it. I better check in and see about the bridge situation."

"All right, be safe out there. If you need anything else, call me. I'll be on the air for the duration. Do you need anything now?"

When Stephen didn't respond, Terrence got worried again. "Hey, you sure you're okay out there? I can send someone to you," Terrence said.

When Stephen still didn't respond, Terrence frowned and breathed in deeply. "Stephen, you there?" Terrence called out, his voice getting louder.

"Yeah, yeah, I'm here. Just checking something out, that's all," Stephen finally returned to the phone to say. "I thought I saw something. I'm not sure."

"Man, you just got out of the hospital a few days ago. You need to take it easy out there. This isn't the kind of weather you need to play with."

"I hear you. I'm fine for real. So how's your lady doing?"

Sherri had been listening to his half of the conversation and had picked up the panic in his voice. He could tell by her expression that she was concerned, as well. He had yet to introduce her to his two best friends, but he would soon.

"You wouldn't believe me if I told you," Terrence said.

At that moment Sherri's own cell phone rang. She pulled it out of her jeans pocket and then stepped outside the room to answer it.

"Sounds serious."

Stephen's words reclaimed Terrence's attention. "It was serious within two minutes after I met her."

"In that case it sounds like the Holy Terror has

finally been tamed. I wish you and your lady the best. Let me know when to get my tux pressed."

Terrence smiled. "Will do. Be safe."

"Back at ya."

Chapter 11

"Yes, Uncle Warrick, everything is fine. Terrence is at the station with me doing weather updates. How are the negotiations going?"

With her uncle's response, a huge smile covered her face. "Uncle Warrick, that's wonderful. We will celebrate when you get back."

Sherri knew the moment Terrence had stepped outside the room, and swung around to face him. Every single nerve in her body became energized. She wished she could put that kiss they'd shared moments ago to the back of her mind, but couldn't.

Her uncle's words pulled her attention back to

their phone conversation. "Terrence? Yes, he's right here. Just a moment."

She handed the phone to Terrence. "Uncle Warrick wants to talk to you." She then went back inside the room to check the monitors.

Terrence watched her walk away before speaking into the phone. "Warrick, this is Terrence."

"Hey, man, I got that station in Memphis. We're going to have to celebrate when I get back."

Terrence chuckled. "Sure thing. I'll spring for the champagne."

"And I want you to watch out for Sherri. Her parents have been calling, freaking out about the hurricane and knowing she's down there in the thick of things. Will you do that for me? Will you make sure she's taken care of?"

A smile touched Terrence's lips. "Don't worry about a thing, Warrick. I can guarantee you that Sherri is in good hands."

"How's your friend?" Sherri asked the moment Terrence walked back into the studio.

"Stephen's fine. The roads are crazy out there, and he wants me to reiterate to everyone to stay inside."

She nodded. "You have less than seven seconds to airtime."

"Thanks." He immediately went to the monitor and sat down. He checked the weather update reel from the Hurricane Center before putting on his headset and turning on the mike. He glanced over at her and smiled before going on the air.

"Hey, folks, this is the Holy Terror. It's time for a weather update. Before I go into the weather, though, I want to again remind everyone to please stay off the roads. Don't go out unless you really have to, and then stick to the evacuation routes. This is not the time to decide you've just got to have a Mr. Goodbar or a Bud Lite. Chances are all the stores in your area are closed anyway."

He leaned back in his chair. "Now for that update on the weather. There has been no change since the last time. It seems Ana doesn't know which way she wants to go and has decided to stall for a while. So, in the meantime, here's another evacuation tip. Think ahead and take video or photos of your property before you leave. This will assist you later with any claims for damages you might need to file. And for heaven's sake, don't forget to take the video or photos with you, and later if you have to turn them in with your claim, make sure you submit the right ones and not the ones taken of you and your old lady skinny-dipping or something else equally intimate."

He glanced over at Sherri, saw her jaw drop and winked at her. "I'm ready to take another call and then you'll be treated to more music after a commercial break."

He clicked a caller on the line. "This is Holy Terror."

Sherri couldn't do anything but shake her head. However, from the callers' comments to Terrence's outlandish take on the evacuation tips, she could see the listeners were actually enjoying it. Go figure.

She stood to stretch her body, knowing his gaze was on her when she went to the window—the portion that wasn't boarded up—and glanced out. Although he had control of the call and was conversing as if the caller's comments had his complete attention, she knew that was not the case.

She had Terrence's complete attention.

She felt it in every part of her body. In every breath she took. When she heard the music start playing again, she knew he would act on all that attention. She wanted to turn around and face him but didn't, not even when she felt the heat of him at her back. He was standing just that close and she almost gasped when he reached out and closed the storm shutters.

She still didn't turn around.

"Sherri."

He spoke her name on a sensual breath that caressed the back of her neck, thrummed warmth through her pores. She didn't want to respond, didn't want her body to react to him, but it was doing so anyway.

"You're an ache inside of me that won't go away unless I'm inside of you. When I'm there, buried deep between your thighs, I'm complete in a way only a woman can make possible for a man. But no other woman will do for me. Only you."

His words were breaking down her control, sweeping her resistance away. They were destroying the last vestige of her sanity. She couldn't fight him any longer because she couldn't stop loving him. Even now, when he could agitate her like nobody's business, she loved him and there was nothing she could do about it.

She slowly turned around. Meeting his dark gaze, she reached out and cupped his face in her hands. He smiled and she lost herself in it. Without any further ado, she leaned up and covered his lips with her own.

Kissing him always did this to her, she thought. Unleashed the feminine desire she'd held closely tethered. When he pulled her closer to the fit of him and she felt his aroused body, that desire broke loose, untamed and undeniable. How could a man make a woman feel this way? So easily, so intensely. From the way his erection was pressed to the apex of her thighs in perfect position, he wanted her, too.

His hand went to her waist, to the snap at her jeans, when the monitor sounded. Muttering a curse, he inhaled deeply and met her gaze. "Don't move," he said before stepping away.

Terrence eased back into his chair and read the blinking monitor. He glanced up at Sherri when she came beside him to read the updated weather alert.

Hurricane Ana was no longer stalling. She was headed straight for the Keys.

Chapter 12

"This is Holy Terror, and I am providing you with the most current weather update that just came in. Hurricane Ana has made her decision and will be making an unwelcome visit to the Keys. Buckle down, folks. It seems we're about to encounter a very wild ride for the next forty-eight hours or so."

He glanced up at Sherri and a wry smile touched his lips as he continued talking into the mike. "If staying with relatives isn't an option, you might want to consider a hotel. Take my advice and book the room. Who wants to stay with relatives at a time like this anyway? Can you imagine trying to get some private time with your old lady with a bunch of relatives around? Go ahead and get the room so you and that special person can bring the hurricane to town right. With all the bumping sounds going on anyway, who will know that the majority of it won't be coming from the outside but from your room? And be smart. Don't tell your relatives what hotel you're going to. They just might show up."

He chuckled when Sherri poked him on the shoulder. Turning off the mike and removing his headset, he unceremoniously pulled her down in his lap and covered her mouth with his. Her resistance lasted all of two seconds and then she was returning his kiss, tangling her tongue with his and blowing away what little control he had.

Breathing heavily, he broke the kiss and stood and then backed her up against the wall. "I need you now."

He pulled her shirt over her head, tossed it aside. And then his hands were on her, kneading her breasts through her lace bra, undoing the front clasp with a flick of the wrist, freeing her breasts for his hands.

Sherri closed her eyes when a responsive shudder shook her body the moment Terrence took a nipple into his mouth, curled his tongue around it and began sucking.

She pulled in a tight breath, felt the stirrings in the

pit of her stomach intensify. Heat flared within her and she felt the moment her panties got wet. She groaned when his mouth went to the other nipple, giving it the same attention and nearly driving her insane in the process.

She was aware of the exact moment his hand reached down to unsnap her jeans. Knew the instant he eased his hand eased inside, finding its way to her hot and ready center.

"I need to taste you first," he murmured while easing down on his knees.

Reaching up, he slid her jeans down past her hips and then down her legs. He helped her out of her shoes and then removed the jeans completely and tossed them aside, and proceeded to do likewise with her panties. When she was totally naked he leaned forward for a moment and buried his face in the juncture of her thighs, as if he needed to consume her scent, feel her heat.

"Terrence."

She breathed his name from her lips when a quiver passed through her.

He slowly raised his head to look at her, and she felt the intensity of his gaze. He seemed to be searching her face, studying every single detail. A seriousness she had never seen before lined his lips.

"Do you have any idea what you do to me?" he asked in a deep, husky voice that was rough and sexy simultaneously. "What you're doing to me now?"

She shook her head. "No. I only know what you did to me. What you're doing to me now."

"And what did I do to you?" he asked, breathing the words hotly against her feminine mound.

She had to tell him. "You gave me pleasure. For the first time in my life, I discovered how things should be with a man and woman in the bedroom. You made me come." There, she figured it couldn't get any clearer than that. He had to understand.

From the smile that suddenly touched his face, the same one that simultaneously touched her heart, she knew that he *had* understood. She'd told him something that he really hadn't needed to know, especially at the risk of escalating his ego, stroking his arrogance. But she had wanted him to know, so he could comprehend what all of this meant to her.

"And I'm going to make you come again. A lot more times. Starting now."

And then he cupped her mound with his hand, opened her up, leaned forward and sank his mouth into her. He licked here, nibbled there, and when she cried out his name he intensified the kiss. She was at a loss to do anything other than let slip her grip on reality, and she groaned in response to the shudders that racked her body.

He didn't let up, nor did he let go. While boneless pleasure ripped through her, his mouth remained latched to her, absorbing everything she had to give, causing her to whimper in pleasure. And when the last shudder shook her body, she opened her eyes and saw he had gotten to his feet and was unzipping his pants.

Time restraints wouldn't allow him to remove them completely, but he was able to push them down past his hips to display his engorged member. He was quick about putting on a condom. Then he gently lifted her off the floor, wrapped her legs around his waist and, meeting her gaze, he rocked his hips against hers, found his target then thrust inside.

She felt him push deep, all the way to the hilt, and she adjusted her body to take him all in. She felt full, and every pore in her body was sensitized to the feelings he had evoked. His body began moving, thrusting in and out of her with whipcord speed, bracing her back against the wall each time he did so.

She fought to hold back the sensations, resist the emotions that took control, but it was no use. Pleasure began overtaking her, shredding her hold on reality and pushing her toward an enormous tide of ecstasy. One more thrust pushed her over, drowning her in sensations.

In response, Terrence screamed her name and held their bodies tight, locked together as quake after quake shook through them, blasting them off the Richter scale. He then leaned forward and kissed her, taking the rest of her trembles in his mouth.

She would no longer deny how she felt, but she couldn't share her feelings with him yet, knowing he didn't feel the same way. For now, this part of their relationship would have to be enough.

"Caller, you're on the line. This is Holy Terror, and this is WLCK. What's going on?"

"Holy Terror, this is Josh. You forgot to take calls after that last weather update and evacuation tip."

Terrence smiled. He hadn't forgotten. He'd gotten into doing something a lot more satisfying. He glanced across the room at Sherri. She met his gaze and a blush tinted her features at the caller's statement. She was pulling back on her jeans. He didn't know why she bothered, since he would be pulling them off her again soon.

"Sorry about that," he said to the caller. "I got sidetracked, but I'm here now. What's on your mind, Josh?"

"Do you think we're going to lose power?"

"I would say count on it, Josh."

"For how long?"

"Hard to say. Could be a couple of days. Remember that no electricity means that the ATMs won't be working, so you need to have some hard cash on hand for any emergencies that might come your way."

"Thanks, I hadn't thought of that. We appreciate the updates out here. You might want to warn your listeners about Domino," Josh said.

Terrence raised a brow. "Domino?"

"Yes, he's a stray dog that roams the streets whenever a bad storm rolls in. You'll be surprised how many female dogs Domino gets pregnant during a storm. So your listeners need to keep any female dogs that aren't fixed behind lock and key or they'll be sorry after Hurricane Ana passes through."

Terrence wondered if the man was serious. "Thanks, Josh, for that advice. Okay, folks, you heard it from Josh, so take heed to his warning. Beware of Domino. And keep in mind that it's unlikely your pet will have a place in a motel or hotel if you decide to check into one. You'll want to find some other place that will keep Fido or Cujo. If you do find a pet-friendly hotel, make sure your cat is blindfolded. If you and your lady decide to get into any action, there's nothing worse than a Peeping Tom." Terrence chuckled, and Sherri rolled her eyes.

"Okay, folks, here's more music. A little bit of Jill Scott will start things off this hour. I'll be back at you in twenty."

After turning off the mike and removing his headset, he looked at Sherri and smiled. "Let's go rob the snack machine. I've gotten hungry."

"So, does your brother have a girlfriend?"

Terrence took a sip of his coffee and then smiled. The employees' lounge didn't have a window and he appreciated not having to see the rain and wind he heard pounding the building. "Why? You're already taken."

Sherri chuckled. "I was thinking of Kim. She needs to meet a real nice guy."

He lifted a brow. "Playing matchmaker?"

"Hey, you aren't so bad, so I figure it might run in the family."

"It does, since I have to admit Duan is a nice person."

Terrence's expression then turned serious. "Duan is also a person who has been burned. That's hard for some men to get over."

"Yes, I would imagine," she said, sipping her own coffee.

"And I understand it's the same way for some women," he decided to throw out there.

Sherri wondered what he was hinting at. How much about her had her uncle shared with him? She sighed. Since she'd already told him that he was the first to give her an orgasm, she figured he deserved the rest of the story, all the boring details.

"Ben was a likable guy. A sweep-you-off-your-feet kind of person. And he definitely swept me off mine. We dated for a year, got engaged and then we moved in together. That's when the problems started. He became needy, wanting all my time, jealous of my work. Then one day over breakfast he told me he didn't want to get married anymore. He accused me of not knowing how to balance my work life and my love life. Unbeknownst to me, he had already packed, and he left, walked out the door a few hours later."

She sighed, remembering that day. "I honestly thought he would be back once he got over it, since he would get pouty at times like a kid. A few days later I discovered he had gotten his own apartment. I got the address and went there and discovered he'd been having an affair. The two of them had already moved in together. I confronted him, and instead of admitting he was the one who had betrayed me, he refused to take accountability and accused me of not giving him the time and attention he deserved."

Terrence reached across the table and lifted her chin up to meet his gaze. "Seems to me that he was the one not giving you the time and attention that *you* deserved."

"I guess we were both wrong for each other. I just didn't see it until too late." She shrugged. "I don't care if I never marry. Sometimes building relationships is too much trouble."

Terrence removed his hand and took another sip of his coffee. "I used to think that very thing, especially seeing how deeply my mother hurt my father when she up and left, committing adultery by running off with another man—a married one at that. You wouldn't believe how many people in our neighborhood knew the story, and their kids had overheard it. I got teased by a good number of them about how no-good my mom was. It made me bitter. I grew up feeling basically like you, not caring if I ever married. Not ever wanting to. But now I believe that not every woman is like my mother. There are women out there who are born to be true mothers, lovers of their man. Trustworthy. Their mate's best friend."

Sherri considered asking when he had figured that

out, but didn't. Instead, while he was in a talkative mood, she said, "Tell me about Stephen. I couldn't help but overhear your conversation with him."

A smile touched his lips, and, as always, it affected her, arousing sensations in her stomach. He had mentioned his two close friends before, Stephen Morales and Lucas McCoy, but he'd never actually said much about them other than they'd gone to college together and were still close. "There isn't anything I wouldn't do for Stephen, or Lucas for that matter. Both of my buddies are single, although Lucas is engaged."

He paused for a moment and then added, "And that concerns me."

Sherri raised a brow. "What concerns you? The fact that he's engaged?"

"No, the fact that I believe he's putting more into this engagement than Emma, his fiancée. It's a long-distance romance, and she seldom comes here. He always has to fly to New York to see her, and when she does say she's coming, she never shows up. Like now. He's expecting her in a few days, once this storm lets up. He wants her to see the house he's building for her. Personally, I doubt she'll come. I told Lucas my feelings on the matter."

"You did?"

"Yes, but it's his decision. I just don't want to see him get taken advantage of."

She nodded. "What about Stephen?"

"His real name is Esteban, but he goes by Stephen and he's single and carefree. He had a few family issues in the past with his father, but now he's doing fine. I'd like for you to meet Stephen and Lucas one day."

"And I would like to meet them," she replied. The fact that he wanted her to meet his best friends meant something, didn't it? Did she want it to mean anything? "And I'd like you to meet Kim."

"I would love to."

She checked her watch. "It's time for another update. And about those evacuation tips…"

He leaned back in his chair and met her gaze. "Yes, what about them?"

She smiled. "I'm beginning to like them."

"Holy Terror, this is Maggie, and what Josh said about Domino is true. The only time I see that mutt is when there's a storm. He got my Mitzy pregnant twice, but they were beautiful puppies. He also got my friend Nancy's dog, Bella, pregnant. He is definitely a rolling stone."

Terrence smiled. "Thanks for sharing that, Maggie. Okay, folks, you heard her. Anyone want to call and describe this famous Casanova on four legs? If you've seen Domino, know how he looks and/or his whereabouts, please call in and let us know."

He clicked on the next call. "This is Holy Terror. What's on your mind?"

"This is Monica. I went to your club, and you didn't show up."

So what does that tell you? he refrained from saying and glanced over at Sherri. She was sitting on the edge of the desk, facing him and listening attentively. "I couldn't make it. I had other things to do. Did you enjoy Club Hurricane?"

"Yes, but it would have been better had you been there."

"But I wasn't. Have you evacuated?"

"I decided to stay put."

"Then stay safe."

He disconnected the call and took another.

Moments later he turned off his mike and removed his headset. It was dark outside, and he glanced at his watch. Nearly eleven o'clock. Time definitely had not stood still.

He stood. "After the music plays, there will be another fifteen minutes of intermittent advertisements, and then that syndicated show from L.A. will kick in until six in the morning. There will be periodic updates directly from the weather station to keep everyone informed. We can chill for a while. Come on," he said, reaching out his hand to her.

She took it. "And just where are we supposed to be going?" There was a hurricane raging out there and she knew he was fully aware of it.

He smiled down at her. "We're going to take a shower and then we're going to bed."

Chapter 13

"This has been a well kept-secret, and now I can see why," Sherri said, glancing around Terrence's office. She met his gaze. "How did you get to be so special around here?" His office included a back room that was actually a studio apartment, complete with a bed, flat-screen TV, an equipped kitchenette, love seat and tables. There was even a bath with a shower.

Terrence chuckled as he pulled off his shirt. "I don't know. You tell me."

Sherri smiled. "I've told you why I think you're special, but why this home away from home? You're seldom here."

He lifted a brow. "Are you sure about that? How often do you come down this particular corridor?"

She shrugged. "Not often. It's too close to Uncle Warrick's office. Whenever he calls, it's the same feeling as when you were summoned to the principal's office. He's my uncle, but his expectations of me are the same as everyone else. I get no special treatment, so I don't like going to his office unless I have to," she said, smiling.

He laughed as he sat on the edge of the bed to take off his shoes. "It can't be that bad, unless you've gotten into trouble."

"Who? Me?" she asked incredulously. "I never get into trouble."

"So you say." He glanced over at her. "Is there any reason you still have your clothes on?" he asked, standing to remove his pants. He then proceeded to roll on a condom.

It always amazed Sherri that he had no qualms about putting on protection in front of her, whereas Ben always retreated to the bathroom, saying it was something a man should do in private. She was glad Terrence didn't think that way because she liked watching him prepare himself for their lovemaking and knowing he cared enough to do it. He had slipped that one time, but she trusted he would be more careful in the future.

She smiled. "Yes, there is a reason I haven't gotten undressed," she finally answered. "I checked out your bathroom. It's nice, but your shower isn't as roomy as mine. It will be a tight fit, so I guess you'll go first."

"Don't hold your breath for that to happen. I like taking showers with you," he said.

"Oh, is that what we did that morning? You could have fooled me."

Completely naked, he crossed the room to her and took her hand and brought it to his lips. "I'd rather make love to you instead. So get out of the clothes. The sooner you do, the sooner we'll both be happy and satisfied. Besides, I want to make love to you lying down this time and not on our feet."

Her eyes twinkled. "I didn't have any complaints."

"Neither did I, but now we have time, and I plan to use it wisely. So, are you going to undress or do you want me to do it?"

"You do it," she challenged.

He grinned. "Gladly."

Terrence began removing her clothes, taking his time and enjoying parts of her body along the way, liking the taste and feel of her skin.

"Do you know what one of my fantasies is regarding you?" he asked, moving his mouth close to her breast. "Taking off your business suit."

She smiled. "I'll make sure I wear one next week just to give you the honor."

Terrence grinned. "I'd like that."

Moments later she said in a breathless voice, "I thought you were in a hurry." He had removed her top but had proceeded to take her breasts into his mouth and torture them the same way he had done earlier.

"I am, but I decided to enjoy myself for a while. Some things you just can't pass up. And I've developed an intense craving for certain parts of your body."

"I can tell," she said, throwing her head back when his mouth moved to the other breast.

It took a while before he got to her jeans, but by the time he had removed them from her, she felt shivers consume her all over. His touch alone could send her over the edge.

Holding her gaze, he reached behind her and gently squeezed her bottom. "Do you know this is the first thing I noticed about you?" he said, murmuring hotly in her ear. "The shape of your backside turned me on that day I walked into Warrick's office and saw you bending over."

She couldn't hold back her grin. "Doesn't take much to turn you on, does it?"

He leaned forward and licked the pulse that was beating at the base of her throat and smiled when he heard her sharp intake of breath. "Just for being a smart-ass, I'm going to see just how much it takes to turn you on."

Her body was naked, fully exposed to his view, and Terrence intended to take her over the edge and back, plenty of times. There was a storm raging outside, and he planned to create his own storm inside.

"You know what they say about payback, right?"

He chuckled. "Yes, I think I've heard once or twice."

"Then get ready to experience it for yourself, Terrence Jefferies."

Before he could take his next breath, she surprised him and went for his mouth, wrapping her arms around his neck and easing her body close to his, feeling the hardness of his erection pressed to her stomach.

She kissed him the way he liked kissing her, using her tongue to touch and find every sensitive spot in his mouth before capturing his tongue with hers and mating intensely.

He was the one who pulled back and quickly turned her in his arms, letting her feel his hard erection against her backside. She was fully aware what he wanted to do, and her senses spiraled out of control at the thought that she would let him.

"Bend over toward the sofa. Grab to it and hold on tight," he instructed, and she did just what he said. He pressed closer to her, reached over and let his hands caress her breasts, moved underneath to touch her stomach and then the juncture of her legs. His fingers found her, touched her, stroked her wetness, and she savored the feel of his hands and the pleasure they were giving her.

"I want to get to this from this way," he whispered in her ear just moments before tilting her behind up, pinning her between him and the sofa. Using his knee, he spread her thighs apart at the same time the palms of his hands splayed across her stomach.

Terrence closed his eyes. The feel of warm bottom pressed against him in perfect position made him quiver, and he inhaled the deep, sensuous scent of her, letting it fill his nostrils. Leaning down, he placed a passion mark on her neck, then another on her back, not caring who might know she was his. It didn't matter. The only thing that mattered was the fact that his heart felt full of love for her and he wanted to mate with her for the rest of his life, this way, in all kinds of ways.

He couldn't last much longer, and he gripped her thighs, brought her body back, closer to the intimate fit of him, and tilted her hips for the perfect angle. Then he entered her. In one long, hard thrust he pushed into her heated warmth.

Sherri gasped at the feel of Terrence deeply embedded inside her body. Holding tight to the sofa, she inhaled deeply. She wished there were mirrors in the room so she could see just how her body was fitting perfectly to his and how deeply connected they were.

She could feel him behind her holding still, not moving an inch, as if he was savoring the feel of being inside her this way, pressing hard against the backside that had turned him on. She glanced over her shoulder and saw his eyes closed, his jaw clenched.

Inside, deep in her body, she felt his engorged member throbbing, waiting for him to move, so she clenched her inner muscles and knew he had felt it from his sharp intake of breath.

"Why did you do that?" he asked in a strained voice.

"To remind you that I'm here," she whispered back.

"Sweetheart, there's no way I could forget." He paused and then said, "I've dreamed about making love to you this way a number of times. If only you knew how many." His grip tightened on the soft cheeks of her backside. "Nice." And then he asked, "Do you feel me?"

The way his staff was throbbing inside her all but had her thighs trembling. She wasn't sure how long she could last. What was he trying to do? Let her anticipation build? If so, it had reached its limit. "Yes, and do you feel me?" she countered, clenching her inner muscles again.

He muttered something, but Sherri wasn't exactly sure what. All she knew was that he had shifted his body again and was beginning to move. She could feel every inch of hard, solid muscle. Heat flared through her with every single stroke, every deep thrust he made, igniting a flame inside her that nearly blazed her brain. The feeling had her calling his name.

The sound made Terrence's nostrils flare, and he inhaled deeply just moments, mere seconds, before he felt her body explode and she jerked, triggering his own body to follow in one earth-shattering release. He gripped her hips tighter, wished at that very moment he was giving her the baby he'd envisioned she would have. Not this time, but he was determined they would share a baby together, after their marriage. Because he would marry her, and it was time she knew it. But first he needed to kiss her.

After the last shudder had touched their bodies, he gathered her into his arms, lifted her up and turned her to him, covering her mouth and thrusting his tongue in deep to mate with hers. He needed the connection. He needed her.

Sweeping her completely into his arms, he broke off the kiss and carried her into the shower. Hurricane Ana was raising a fury of problems outside, but here on the inside, he was a very happy, satisfied man.

Sherri's movement woke Terrence. His thigh was thrown over hers and she'd been trying to ease out of bed.

"Where do you think you're going?" he asked in a sleepy tone of voice, nuzzling her neck.

"To the bathroom, and then to check to see if the weather has changed," she whispered.

"Let it go for now, Sherri. If there's an alert, we'll get a call. Stay in bed with me."

"All right. But only if you at least let me go to the bathroom," she teased.

He loosened his hold on her, and she turned on the lamp and then quickly scooted out of the bed, shivering as she hurried across the room. The air conditioner was on full blast, and she guessed in a way she should appreciate the station's generators. She was certain in some parts of town some residents didn't have any power.

Returning, she decided to borrow one of Terrence's T-shirts. She glanced over at him, glad he had gone back to sleep. She moved quietly across the room to the dresser and opened the top drawer. Instead of clothing, all she saw was papers. She was about to push the drawer closed when something caught her eye. Picking the document up, she held it close to the light.

Shock and disbelief tore through her, and she closed her eyes to fight back tears. Why hadn't anyone told her? Why didn't she know?

Turning back to the bed, she studied Terrence's features as he slept. At that moment, she felt a sense of betrayal. Glancing around, she quickly saw her clothes scattered all about. There was no way she could leave due to the weather, but at least she could go stay in her office until the roads were clear. She continued looking for one of Terrence's T-shirts and found one that suited her. Slipping it over her naked body, she picked up her clothes and bundled them together and left the room. She fought back the tears as she made it to her office and locked the door. For now she needed to be alone.

Terrence shifted in bed and found the spot beside him empty. He opened his eyes, remembering Sherri had left the bed to go to the bathroom, but that had been a while ago. Where was she? Had she gone to the studio when he had told her there was no need for her to do so?

Getting out of bed, he slipped into his jeans and left his office to head down the long hallway. She wasn't in the studio, and from the look of things, she hadn't been there. He frowned as he made his way back to his office, thinking she might very well have been in the bathroom.

He was about to pass her office when he noticed the light on underneath the door. He tried the door and found it locked. He knocked gently. "Sherri, are you in there?"

"Yes. Go away. I don't have anything to say to you."

Terrence quirked a confused brow. After making love, they had taken a shower, made love in the shower, then gone to bed and made love again. They had fallen asleep in each other's arms, happy and satisfied. What had happened from that time to now? He had never been one to do stupid things in his sleep, at least not that he was aware of. Hell, he needed to be sure.

"What happened, Sherri? What's wrong?"

"Just leave me alone. I don't want to talk to you."

The hell she wouldn't talk to him! He went to his office and got the master key to every door at the station, then returned to open Sherri's door.

From the look on her face, he had caught her by surprise. She'd swung around from where she'd been standing by the window and he couldn't help but notice how good she looked in his Miami Dolphins T-shirt that hit her midthigh.

"I told you I didn't want to talk to you."

Her words grabbed his attention, and he moved his gaze off her legs and to her face. He could tell she'd been crying. "That's tough," he said, crossing the room to her. "We're going to talk, because I want to know what I did to make you leave my bed."

"I don't have anything to say to you, and as soon as the weather clears, I'm leaving."

He crossed his arms over his chest. "No, you're not. Look out that window again, baby. Hurricane Ana hasn't officially arrived yet, and you see how things look. If you think for one minute I'd let you go out in that storm, then you have another thought coming."

Anger flared in her face. "You don't own me. I was just someone you slept with. You lied to me. Uncle Warrick lied to me. All men are nothing but liars," she all but screamed.

Terrence just stared at her. She wasn't making sense. "What the hell are you talking about?"

"I'm talking about the fact that I went into your top drawer to look for a T-shirt and found out the truth, Terrence. Uncle Warrick doesn't own WLCK. You do."

Chapter 14

Terrence blew out a breath. "Is that what got you upset?" he asked, clearly not understanding what the problem was even if he did own the station.

"Well, is it true? Do you own it?" she asked, glaring at him.

"What does it matter who owns the station?" he asked, throwing up his hands.

She crossed the room to stand in front of him. "Because whoever owns it is my boss, and I don't take kindly to the idea of sleeping my way to the top."

"So are you saying that if I'm the owner and not

Warrick, then you would never have gone out with me? Shared a bed with me?"

"Of course I would not have!" she snapped. "Just think of the ethics involved. What would people think?"

He narrowed his gaze. "Frankly, I don't give a royal damn what people think. And as far as my ownership of WLCK, it's merely on paper. For all intents and purposes, Warrick is the owner. As a favor to him, I'm holding the mortgage."

"And why didn't someone tell me?" she spat out.

A deep frown lined Terrence's face. "Frankly, because it wasn't any of your business. It was a business deal between me and Warrick. He needed extra cash flow, and this was the way to do it. It didn't concern you or anyone here at the station."

"No wonder you've been getting special treatment," she said as if his explanation meant nothing to her. "It all makes sense now. You report to no one but Uncle Warrick, you make your own hours, you have this plush office. And on top of everything, you're sleeping with the hired help. Is that how you get your kicks?"

Her words were like a slap to his face. Terrence stared at her for a moment and then asked, "Is that what you think? Do you think I slept with you because you're available and all it meant to me was a fun time in bed?"

When she didn't say anything, he continued. "That says a lot for what you think of me, Sherri. And to think I fell in love with you the first time we made love."

"What?"

"You heard me. But I guess you wouldn't believe something like that, either, since I'm such a horrid person."

"You can't love me. Men like you don't fall in love."

"If you truly believe that, then I guess men like me really don't." Without saying anything else, Terrence turned and walked away.

"This is Holy Terror and I am providing you with the most current weather update that just came in. Hurricane Ana is still a Category One, and if you were hoping that overnight she would have changed her mind and shifted positions, I'm sorry to say that didn't happen. Although I'm sure you won't be putting out the welcome mat, you can expect her late tonight. WLCK is committed to bringing you periodic updates. And we want you to stay off the roads as much as possible. We're getting heavy winds and rain with zero visibility. We'll take a few calls after a couple of announcements from our sponsors."

Terrence clicked off the mike, took off his headset and leaned back in his chair. It was close to noon, and he had yet to see Sherri. She was holed up in her office. Thank God she had more sense than to go out in this weather, no matter how angry she was with him. An anger he considered unjustified.

He felt his cell phone vibrate in his pocket and stood to pull it out. It was Lucas. "Hey, man, how are things going?"

"Fine. I'm just hoping the weather improves and the airport reopens. I'm expecting Emma to arrive when things clear."

Terrence rolled his eyes. "And you're really expecting her this time?"

"I know you and Stephen think she isn't serious about coming and—"

"After a number of no-shows, do you blame us?" Terrence paused, then said, "You're building that house for her, and she hasn't been to see it, not once. I don't want you to get your hopes up and be disappointed."

Lucas gave a dry chuckle. "It won't be the first time with Emma." After a brief moment, he said, "I know you're stuck at the station, so when the weather clears how about dropping by for breakfast?"

"Thanks, I'd like that."

"Good. How are things going with you and Miss WLCK?"

"Don't ask."

Lucas laughed. "You're losing your touch, man."

"Possibly, but she's not like the others. I've fallen in love, and I've fallen hard."

"You?"

"Yes, me. The only thing is that she doesn't believe it."

"Why not? You're certainly not someone who'd claim to love a woman when he doesn't."

"Evidently she doesn't think so," Terrence said, tossing a pencil on the table.

"Well, I guess you're going to have to work on her some more."

"That's not going to happen. If she doesn't take my word for it then that's too bad."

"Sounds like the both of you are stubborn. That's not good," Lucas said. "Well, I guess I'll call and check on Stephen. I'll talk to you again later."

"Okay."

Terrence clicked off the phone and put it back into his pocket. He glanced at the monitor and slid his headset back on and clicked on the mike.

"Welcome back, folks. This is the Holy Terror,

and I'm ready to take call number one. You're up, Cheryl. What's on your mind?"

Sherri leaned back in her chair and listened to Cheryl as she recounted how bad things were in her neighborhood.

Like some others, Cheryl had not evacuated, deciding to ride out the storm and remain in her home. Now she wished she had left. All the streets around her were flooded, and one of her neighbor's trees had fallen on her husband's toolshed. But Cheryl was thankful no one had gotten hurt.

Sherri had to grudgingly admit that Terrence had a way with people. He had a personality that made anyone feel comfortable in talking to him. He had taken several calls this morning, more than he had taken yesterday. Some had been sad and some amusing, and in the midst of a killer storm he was doing his best to keep things upbeat, especially with all those crazy calls regarding the now-famous Domino.

Sherri went to the window and lifted the storm shutter so she could look out. She hadn't realized it had gotten so late. Other than going to the snack machine and grabbing a couple of sodas and snack food, she had remained in her office, hoping she didn't run into Terrence.

She moved her neck around, trying to get the kinks out. She had slept the rest of the night in her chair and awakened with her body feeling abused. It was around four in the afternoon and already it was getting dark. Terrence was still encouraging the listeners to stay inside, and she hoped they did what he asked.

She turned when her cell phone rang and quickly walked back over to her desk to pick it up. "Hello."

"It's Kim, just checking in. The hospital is a zoo. We've been pretty busy all night. This is the first time I've taken a break. How are you and Holy Terror handling things?"

"Professionally, fine. We're keeping everyone informed how the weather is doing."

"And personally?"

Sherri took a deep breath, and she dropped down in her chair. "I think I screwed up."

"How?"

"I found out that Terrence holds the mortgage on the radio station."

"And?"

Sherri rolled her eyes. "And no one told me. If he's the owner, then technically he's my boss. I've slept with him. Ben was sleeping with one of his employees and—"

"Will you forget about Ben? The man betrayed

you. Get over it, Sherri. Are you going to mess up something that can possibly lead to something good because your ex-fiancé couldn't be trusted? And I don't care who he chose as his bed partner when he screwed around on you. It doesn't matter. As far as I'm concerned, good riddance. You've said so yourself."

Yes, she had. "I love him, you know."

"Who? Ben?"

"No, not Ben. Not anymore. I'm beginning to wonder if I ever did love him. I love Terrence. I didn't want to fall in love with him. I fought it like hell, but it happened anyway."

She paused a moment and then said, "And last night he told me he loved me, too. And that was after I said some mean things to him."

"Let me get this straight. The Holy Terror, Terrence Jefferies, actually said that he loved you?"

"Yes."

"Dang. Do you believe him?"

"At first, no, but now that I've had time to think about it, yes, I believe him. And he was right. What was between him and Uncle Warrick was a business deal that doesn't concern me. No one else at the station knows about it, and evidently they wanted to keep it that way."

"And how did you find out?" Kim asked.

"Last night, I got cold and went through his drawer looking for a T-shirt, saw the paper and read it."

"He could have said something to you about invading his privacy," Kim pointed out.

"Yes, he could have, but he didn't. I guess he was too upset to think about it at the time."

"Well," Kim said, "my break is over and I need to get back to work. Seems like you have a lot to clean up with Terrence. Good luck. When all this is over, you and I need to sit down and talk."

"All right, and if things work out with me and Terrence, I'll introduce you to his brother one day. I've seen a picture of him. He's a hunk."

Kim laughed. "Trying to play matchmaker?"

"Yeah, but I need to take care of my own business first. Like you said, clean things up. I don't know how Terrence feels about me now."

"There's only one way to find out," Kim said teasingly. "Some people think the way to a man's heart is through his stomach. I personally think the area is a tad lower than that."

"Hey folks, this is Holy Terror, and it's time for your weather update. Hurricane Ana is kicking butt, and the Keys are taking a beating. The authorities think the worst is yet to come and are asking everyone to stay inside and do whatever you need to stay safe. I hope you've stocked up on water and propane gas, because you're going to need it. And I understand some of you don't have power and are listening to me on battery-powered radios. Be careful with those candles."

He looked at the monitor. "We're going to take a commercial break, after which we'll take a few calls. Hang tight."

Terrence turned off the mike, removed his headset and pushed away from the table. He suddenly picked up Sherri's scent regardless of the fact he didn't see her anywhere. He glanced at the door, expecting her. It didn't take too long for her to appear. It was almost six in the evening and the first time he'd seen her all day.

She looked good. Refreshed. Sexy.

She was wearing another pair of jeans, a darker denim than yesterday, and her polo shirt today was black instead of blue. She met his gaze the moment she walked through the door and stood in the middle of the room for a second. He watched as she took a deep breath before strolling over to where he sat.

"Terrence."

"Sherri."

"Can we talk?"

He glanced at the monitor. "Not now. I'm about to take a few calls."

She glanced at the monitor. "I'll wait."

"Suit yourself." Whatever she had to say, he wasn't going to make it easy on her. Trust was important in any relationship, and her actions earlier proved that although they had spent time together, slept together, she still didn't trust him.

Instead of taking the chair, she began pacing, and although he tried not to focus on her, he did so anyway. He noticed how good she looked in her jeans. How curvy her backside was in them. He then remembered that backside that he branded his last night and memories of how he had done so sent trembles through his body, made him hard.

Fighting the feeling, he turned his attention to the monitor. He had three calls holding.

"Hey, folks, this is Holy Terror, and I'm ready to take those calls. First up is Ray. What's on your mind?"

"Hey there, Holy Terror. Enjoying the music. Me and my old lady took your advice and checked into a hotel. Nice. I just wanted to let the listeners know that I saw Domino, and he had a lady friend. If anyone is missing a female Black Lab, then it might be too late."

Terrence couldn't help but smile. "Hey, Ray, thanks for letting us know." He disconnected the line. "Next caller, you're up. What's on your mind?"

Sherri stopped pacing and glanced over at Terrence. He was deliberately not looking at her, and that was okay for now, but she refused to let him ignore her once he had finished taking those calls. She'd admit that she had been wrong to get into his business, and she would apologize and hope he would forgive her. But then she and Terrence needed to do something they hadn't really done. Talk about their feelings for each other. She hadn't known he had fallen in love with her, just like he didn't know she had fallen in love with him.

She wanted to continue to build a relationship if that's what he wanted, and she hoped that it was. But what if it wasn't? What if he wasn't willing to forgive her? With those uncertainties, she began pacing again.

When Terrence finished with the last call, he glanced over at Sherri. Their eyes met, and he was consumed with memories of all the pleasure they had shared last night. But then, that pleasure had been tossed aside by her harsh words.

He pushed back in his chair. "You want to talk, go ahead."

He watched her inhale deeply before she came closer to the table where he sat. "I need to explain why I went off the way I did. It has to do with Ben."

When he didn't say anything, but continued to look at her, she continued. "I told you that Ben broke our engagement because of another woman. What I didn't tell you was that the other woman was someone who worked for him, wanted to bang her way to the top. I detested her for it, and I loathed Ben as an employer for letting her do it. In my mind a person who would do such a thing was unethical, undeserving. And last night, I became that sort of woman when I found out you're the boss and I was sleeping with you."

"I am not the boss," he said in an angry tone. "Let's get that straight right now, Sherri. And like I said, this is a business deal between me and Warrick and doesn't concern you or anyone else who works at this station. Now that things have worked out with Warrick and that station in Memphis, he'll have the financial package he needs to get back control of things."

She nodded. "I understand, and I want to apologize for everything I said last night. You said you love me. Well, I got one up on you, Terrence, because I love you, too."

She lifted her chin. "And I didn't just fall in love with you when we made love. I loved you before then. I just didn't want to admit it. In all honesty, I tried denying it to the hilt. But I can't any longer. I've realized that loving you is right."

He didn't say anything for a long moment, and then, "You said you didn't believe I loved you because men like me didn't fall in love. What did you mean by that?"

She glanced down at the floor and then back at him. "Within a week of coming to town, I found out about your reputation as a ladies' man, Terrence. You're one of the most eligible bachelors in the Keys. Women call the station just to flirt with you. They go to your club just to get a glimpse of you. You're an ex-pro-football player. Handsome. Intelligent. Wealthy. You've dated celebrities. Why would a man give that up—the life of a bachelor—to fall in love with anyone? And why me?"

Slowly getting out of his chair, Terrence crossed the room to stand in front of her. He studied her features. "You might want to be asking this question. Why *not* you?"

He gave her a moment for that question to sink in and then he said, "You're beautiful. Intelligent. A career woman who knows what she wants and doesn't mind working hard to achieve it." He paused a second. "You're also a woman who has made me feel things I've never felt before, at least not with the same magnitude. When I'm inside of you, I don't want to come out. You're the only woman that I've envisioned having a baby with. The only woman I allowed access to my heart. So I'm no different from any other man, Sherri. I want love just like the next guy, and I want to think I'm smart enough to recognize it when it comes along and take a chance."

She tried fighting back the tears, but one fell down her cheek anyway. She quickly swiped it away. "So, do you accept my apology?"

"Only if you promise never to doubt my love for you again."

She smiled through the tears in her eyes. "I promise."

"Then I accept your apology."

He leaned in and brushed her lips with his. "I just thought of something that I need to do."

Sherri watched as he walked back to the monitor and took a seat. A commercial break was going on, which would be followed by nonstop music for at least an hour. She lifted a brow when she realized he was about to interrupt and do an unscheduled station alert of some sort right after the commercial.

He turned on the mike and slipped into his headset.

"This is Holy Terror in a very special appeal. This is for all the lovers out there weathering the storm in each other's arms. Tonight is the night not to tell, but to show that special someone how you feel about them. So, brothers, while Hurricane Ana is out there banging on the door, you take care of your business and take your special lady in your arms. Give her love. Show her how much you care. And, ladies, you know what to do. Me, well, let's just say I'm doing just fine right here."

Not realizing he hadn't turned off the mike, he looked over to Sherri and said, "Come here, baby, let's get it on."

Sherri smiled and walked over to him. Her smile widened as she clicked off the mike, removed his headset and slid into his lap just as Marvin Gaye's classic "Let's Get It On" began bathing the airwaves in a melodic and soulful sound.

"I love you," she whispered against his lips.

"And I love you," he whispered against hers.

And then it was on.

He hungrily took her mouth, and her response was immediate. His tongue moved thoroughly and methodically inside of her mouth, showing her the love, making her feel it. She was his and he was hers and that's how things would always be.

Moments later when he raised his head and looked into her eyes, he knew he was seeing his future, the woman who would be his wife, the mother of his children, his soul mate, helpmate, his lover for all eternity.

He stood with her in his arms and headed for the special private haven in his office. Hurricane Ana could do as she pleased, but in the meantime, he intended to take care of business with the woman he loved by putting his own advice into practice.

This was going to be one storm that he'd never forget.

* * * * *

Don't miss Duan Jefferies's story,
SPONTANEOUS,
coming in May 2010
from Harlequin Blaze.

KIMANI™
ROMANCE